All Because of a DOG CALLED LUCKY

JUDITH SPENCER

BALBOA.PRESS
A DIVISION OF HAY HOUSE

Balboa Press books may be ordered through booksellers or by contacting:

Balboa Press
A Division of Hay House
1663 Liberty Drive
Bloomington, IN 47403
www.balboapress.co.uk
UK TFN: 0800 0148647 (Toll Free inside the UK)
UK Local: (02) 0369 56325 (+44 20 3695 6325 from outside the UK)

Print information available on the last page.

ISBN: 978-1-9822-8843-3 (sc)
ISBN: 978-1-9822-8844-0 (hc)
ISBN: 978-1-9822-8842-6 (e)

Library of Congress Control Number: 2024905203

Balboa Press rev. date: 05/13/2024

To my wonderful family whom I love dearly.

Contents

One

It was a warm and sunny morning in May 1877 when Fred Lee decided to visit his aunt Ann to discuss a matter which was weighing heavily on his mind. He had thrashed about in his bed the night before, turning the problem over and over in his mind but getting no closer to finding the answer. At last, as the dawn was breaking, he had remembered his dear aunt, who was such a sensible soul, thinking that she would be sure to help him if anyone could do so. He heaved a great sigh, turned on his side, and managed to fall asleep for a couple of hours.

"Wake up, Fred!" boomed a voice in his ear. "Breakfast is ready, and your mother doesn't want it to get cold."

Fred opened his eyes and looked towards the open door, where his father, Frederick Senior, was standing. Frederick worked on the railways. He had a bushy beard and an impressive moustache and would occasionally joke that all his hair had dropped downwards because his head was as bald as an egg. He was a larger-than-life character, full of good cheer and optimism, quite certain that better times were just around the corner. It was his latest scheme that was causing his son, Fred, so much mental anguish, although he was either unaware of the fact or chose to ignore the matter.

"I'll be along in a minute, Pa," said Fred, as he struggled upright and swung his legs to the ground, "but I really don't feel very hungry this morning. Please, would you tell Ma that I will just have some porridge? If you don't need me this morning, there is something I have to do."

Giving his son a quizzical look, Frederick replied, "Well, it's a Sunday and your free day. The family will be going to chapel in an hour, but I can see from your face that you think you have more pressing matters on your mind."

"Indeed I have," Fred answered. "I really don't think you're aware, Pa, that I'm very worried about your plans for the future. I just can't share your enthusiasm, and I'm full of doubt and concern, so I'm going to visit Aunt Ann to seek her advice."

"In that case," said Frederick, "I suggest you be on your way as soon as possible because it will take you at least three hours to walk there. And although the sun is shining now, the clouds will build up later and there will be rain before nightfall."

Fred splashed his face with the cold water in the bowl on his nightstand and proceeded to dress in his most comfortable clothes. He decided against the cumbersome business of shaving, and anyway, at the age of twenty, there wasn't anything more than a little fluff on his chin. Very eager to be on his way, he almost missed eating his porridge, until his mother remonstrated, "I'll not let you out of this house until you've finished that bowlful. You need sustenance for your walk. I know your aunt will provide you with some food when you arrive, but you need something inside you now."

At last Fred was on his way. He was almost running in his eagerness to reach his destination, but common sense made him slow down to a brisk walk. He began to enjoy the fresh, warm air and the scenery, which was simply beautiful at this time of year. Meadowsweet and buttercups grew in great profusion along the sides of the country lanes, and the heavenly scent of bluebells filled the air. Having climbed a steep hill, he could see the shimmer of the sea in the distance and calculated that he had about another hour before arriving at the small village where his aunt and uncle lived.

A rider on his horse paused to greet him. "Good morning, young fellow. What a lovely day it is!" before trotting off in the opposite direction.

There were surprisingly few people about, and Fred guessed it was because most of them, being God-fearing folk, were in church. He had the rather profound thought that he would rather worship his God in the open air, marvelling at all the miracles around him.

In was thus in a rather contemplative mood that Fred passed the next half hour, until he was suddenly aware that he was being followed by a very scruffy dog. "Hello, old chap," he said, stooping down to give the dog a pat. "And where have you sprung from? You look thirsty. Come to think of it, I'm rather dry myself. Shall we share a drink?" He felt in his pocket for the flask which his mother had pressed upon him and took a long refreshing drink before pouring some water into his cupped hands and offering it to his companion. The dog gladly lapped it up before turning adoring eyes upon Fred and wagging his tail furiously. He seemed to be a strange mix of breeds. His filthy fur looked as if it should be white, but it was dull and very matted, and the creature was painfully thin. He was about the size of a spaniel but had longer legs, and his ears were very odd indeed as one stuck up straight whilst the other flopped down. "Go home now, boy," commanded Fred. "You can't come any further with me." The dog, however, had other ideas. As much as Fred tried to shoo him off, the dog stayed obstinately by his side.

Aunt Ann and her family lived in a small village just west of Southampton. As Fred neared the town, the traffic began to increase. There were carts and carriages and people on horseback, and altogether the noise was fairly deafening. Fred could hear the distant whistle of a train leaving the station, and far out at sea a great liner was leaving the port for distant countries with steam pouring out of its multiple funnels. All this was quite exciting to a young man who had lived a fairly sheltered existence, but the dog hated it and clung even more closely to Fred's side, panting and rolling his eyes in distress.

"You poor thing," Fred said sympathetically, bending down to give him a comforting pat. "You don't like this at all, do you? It won't last long. We'll soon be out on the country roads again for the last mile into Colbury. It looks as if you're going to follow me wherever

I go, so I'm thinking I'll have to give you a name. How does 'Lucky' sound to you? Because, you know, you were very lucky when you chose me as your companion, because anyone else would have kicked you away right from the start."

Having once again turned off into a grassy lane edged with wild flowers, Fred began to hum a tune, and Lucky visibly relaxed. They strolled companionably along the last two hundred yards of the road, and at last Aunt Ann's cottage came into view. Despite its being a Sunday, Fred could see a line of clean washing flapping in the breeze and could hear the sounds of his young cousins playing in the small but tidy garden. Aunt Ann, who had spotted her nephew coming up the lane, was standing at the door to welcome him.

"My dear, how wonderful to see you! Come in, come in. Is your dog safe? He doesn't bite, does he? What brings you here? Are your parents well?"

Fred laughed and, holding up his hands, replied to this rather breathless greeting, saying, "Good morning, Aunt. This is Lucky. And no, he won't bite. In fact, he seems to be the kindest, most loyal dog you could wish for. And my parents are well, thank you. As to why I'm here, I will explain in a minute once I have sat down and perhaps enjoyed some of that excellent lemonade you always keep in your larder."

"Of course," said Ann. "Where are my manners? You sit down, and I will fetch you a drink. I don't doubt that the children would like one too. And then, because it's such a lovely day, you stay there and relax in the sunshine while I find you something to eat. I have some excellent cheese and pickles just waiting for a hungry lad like you." Ann whisked off indoors, leaving Fred to contemplate how to raise the reason for his visit. He wondered if his uncle William was at home or if he had slipped down to the local brickworks where he was employed, despite its being a Sunday and officially his day off.

Ten minutes later, Ann was back, laden with drinks and great chunks of fresh bread, cheese, and pickles. There was also a bowl of water and the remains of a cooked rabbit for Lucky, which disappeared in seconds.

"Your dog seems to be very hungry," remarked Ann. "Hasn't he eaten anything today?" Fred explained in a few words how Lucky had come to be with him. "You have a kind heart, my dear. Now you refresh yourself, and then you can tell me what brings you here."

The children were summoned for their lemonade but soon lost interest in their cousin and returned to their games, whilst Ann, who could no longer contain her curiosity, burst out with, "So, Fred! What's all this about? You've been sitting there with such a heavy look on your face that I fear it's not good news."

"No, Aunt," Fred replied, "it's something that has been deeply worrying me. You see, it's about the latest scheme my father has thought up, and this time I'm convinced he is serious and will carry it through."

"Well, we all know your father," said Ann, "and we know it's a fact that in no time at all he'll have lost interest in whatever the current plan may be."

"Not this time, Aunt. He has decided that our whole family is going to emigrate to New Zealand. The railway system out there is still very new, and he is quite sure he will find employment. He is so full of enthusiasm and is utterly convinced that we will make a fortune out there. Ma has no choice but to agree with him. And my four sisters, well, being so much younger than me, they are all very excited about the picture he has painted."

Ann lifted her hand to her mouth and cried out in horror, "Oh no! He can't do this! For one thing, it's taking such a risk. He may not find a job as easily as he thinks, and then where will you all be? And it's so very far away. We will never see any of you again, and I can't bear the thought of that. Is there nothing you can do to dissuade him? Oh, Fred, this is awful."

"I know," replied Fred, reaching out to hold his aunt's hand. "I really don't want to go with them," he admitted. "I love England, and I feel my future lies here. I already have a job as a trained carpenter, so why should I want to go off to the other side of the world and maybe end up unemployed? I'm of a mind to disobey my father and refuse to go. I can, you know. I'm going to be twenty-one in October, an adult in the eyes of the law, able to make my own decisions. As for Pa, I'll do my best, but his mind seems to be made up, and he shrugs off any other argument or point of view."

Ann began to cry and wring her hands in despair. "I will write to him," she said. "Perhaps he will listen to me, although I very much fear that any pleas from me will fall on deaf ears. I know my brother too well."

At this moment, William strode into the garden and looked with puzzlement at his nephew and his wife, the latter of whom was obviously in great distress. "Whatever is this?" he demanded. "Has anything happened to your family, Fred?"

"No, but I did come to visit you with some disturbing news. I will leave it to Aunt Ann to explain because I must be on my way before it gets too dark to see my path. Come, Lucky! Goodbye, Aunt and Uncle William. I'll visit again when I have more news." With this he hurriedly rose from his seat, walked down the garden path, and went through the gate. He gave one last look back and saw that William had his arm round Ann's shoulders in an effort to comfort her as she sobbed her heart out.

Two

The journey home seemed endless as Fred mulled the situation over and over again in his mind without reaching any conclusion. He very much doubted that the promised letter from Aunt Ann to her brother would have any effect at all. Lucky continued to plod along by his side, occasionally brushing up against him as if to give support, and in a strange way it did seem to provide a small measure of comfort.

Dusk was beginning to fall and there was moisture in the air as Fred finally arrived back home. The family lived in a small rented cottage in the village of Warsash, a few miles east of the River Hamble. Frederick Lee and his wife, Matilda, always considered themselves very fortunate that they could afford such comfortable accommodation. True, there were only three bedrooms, the largest of which was used by their four small daughters, Edith, Annie, Mary, and Esther, whilst Fred slept in little more than a cupboard. However, they also enjoyed the luxury of an inside privy, and Matilda was the envy of her friends in the village, who still had to use a rather malodorous little outbuildings in their backyards.

"I'm back," called out Fred as he pushed open the door leading into the hall. To the left of this was the parlour, used only for visitors and special occasions, whilst on the right was the comfortable all-purpose room where the family was to be found when they were at home. Adjoining this was a small scullery where Matilda cooked all the meals for her family, attended to the huge weekly wash, and tackled all manner of domestic chores. During the cold winter months, there would be a huge blazing fire in the living room, fuelled by logs and wood collected by Fred and his father from the surrounding countryside. Today, however, there was the merest glimmer to take the chill off the evening air. Fred's father was seated in an old leather chair, peacefully smoking his pipe; his sisters were engaged at the table in a noisy game of cards; and his mother was busy preparing the cold meal which was customary on a Sunday evening.

They all turned at the sound of Fred's voice. Then Matilda shrieked, "What's that you've got with you? Fred, you know I can't abide dogs! Get it out of here! It's filthy dirty and is probably covered with fleas. How could you, Fred? Send it on its way this minute." The four small girls, on the other hand, had left their game and were crouched on the floor patting Lucky's back and tickling him under the chin. The dog further enchanted them by extending his paw.

"I'm sorry, Ma," said her rather unrepentant son, "but he attached himself to me quite early on in my walk to Colbury. And I must confess that I have really grown rather fond of him. I'll take him out into the backyard and give him a good washdown, after which I'm sure he would appreciate something to eat and drink because, as you can see, he looks half-starved. Oh, by the way, I've called him Lucky."

Frederick had remained silent during all this, puffing on his pipe and staying firmly in his chair, but now he began to speak. "I can understand how you feel, Son. You have had a very long walk today, and it's lonely on your own. Wash and feed the dog by all means, but then he will have to go. He managed before you came along, and he will manage again. These strays can be very self-sufficient. After all, he can't come to New Zealand with us, so it's best for him to go now before anyone"—he nodded towards his four young daughters—"becomes too attached to him."

It was as if a bright light had suddenly shone in Fred's brain at his father's solemn pronouncement of "The dog can't come to New Zealand." *Well, then,* he thought, *I won't go either.* He felt almost light-headed at his sudden decision, but he knew without any doubt whatsoever that it was the right one to make. He would not accompany his family to the other side of the world. He would stay in England with Lucky and make his own life in the country he loved.

Fred's imagination began to soar, until he was brought back to earth by his father's exclaiming, "Well, what are you waiting for? Go outside and wash the creature. I'm sure your mother will be able to find some scraps for him to eat when he is clean and free of any vermin, but then he will have to go." He turned his head away, pretending to ignore the reproachful looks from his small daughters.

Putting aside his momentous decision for the moment, Fred realised that his biggest task now would be to persuade his parents to let Lucky stay with him for the next few weeks. "Come on, boy," he said. "Let's clean you up so they can see what a handsome lad you are under all that dirt." He moved towards the door leading to the backyard, and Lucky immediately followed him outside. By now night had fallen and it was raining heavily. "That's useful," remarked Fred to his faithful friend. "Now I won't have to carry buckets of water out here to wash. We can just stand here and let the rain do the job. I must say, I feel almost as unkempt as you are, Lucky."

Three

Fred awoke the next morning feeling more relaxed than he had in many weeks. He instantly realised that after so much fretting, his calmer, happier mood was the result of the decision he had made the previous evening. Giving a huge sigh of relief, he acknowledged to himself there was a difficult task ahead when confronting his father with his decision, but nevertheless he was absolutely sure that it was the right thing to do.

Suddenly, Fred was aware of two bright eyes and a quivering nose just inches away from his face. *Lucky! Of course! He must need to go outside.* Fred jumped out of bed and went out to the backyard, only to discover it was still pouring with rain, which on one hand was a good thing because he could use it as an excuse to keep the dog for another night. On the other hand, however, he had a four-mile walk to reach his place of work, and try as he might to keep dry on days like this, the rain always managed to give him a thorough soaking.

Fred had been a fairly latecomer to his chosen profession as a carpenter, having only recently completed his apprenticeship at the age of twenty, whereas the usual age was seventeen. Being the only boy in the family, he had been somewhat indulged by his ma and pa when it came to deciding on his future employment, and once he had left school at the age of fourteen, he had been allowed to try several options. Thus, he had helped a local farmer during his busy season by bringing in the hay for the winter, only to find that the process affected his breathing and made him very wheezy. Then he manned a stall selling eggs and vegetables at the weekly market held in the local town, but this earned him very little money and could never be termed a career. He was a bright, industrious boy, and his parents had even discussed the possibility of his training to become a teacher. After all, he was very patient with his younger sisters, and he could read extensively, write legibly, and do calculations in his head without making any mistakes. However, money was short, so they had agreed it was time for Fred to settle down in an occupation which would benefit the whole family now and not at some time in the future.

At the age of twelve, Fred had come across a battered wooden crate and had lovingly fashioned it into a quite passable sidetable. Eventually, that one incident encouraged him to take up carpentry. Now, at the age of twenty, he was one of a small team of men working together and was beginning to make a name for himself throughout the local community.

He contemplated all this during his walk that morning and wondered, now that his decision was made, how his future in England would unfold. Occasionally he glanced down to make sure that Lucky was still trotting along by his side. He had no qualms about taking Lucky to work with him, knowing that the dog would behave as long as he could stay near him. And anyway, Fred's boss would not be able to remonstrate because he had a cat that followed him to work every day and prowled around the workshop, frequently catching the ever-present rats and mice.

"G'd morning, Fred," the gaffer greeted upon his arrival at the workplace. "Take off that wet coat and have a nice hot cup of tea before we start. You can't do a good job when you're in that state. This rain won't go on much longer, and when the sun comes out, you can dry your coat off outside." He then seemed to notice Fred's companion for the first time. "And who's this then?"

"His name is Lucky," replied Fred. "It's a long story, and I'll tell you all about it when we're on our lunch break. I'm very much hoping you don't mind Lucky staying with me while I work. He's very obedient, and he won't be a nuisance."

Fred anxiously waited for his chief's reaction to his plea. He was relieved to hear him say, "As long as he doesn't trouble my cat or get in anybody's way, then he can stay. But at the first sign of any problem, he will have to be tied up outside until you take him home."

Now that he was a fully fledged carpenter, Fred was given the responsibility of training a young apprentice by the name of James. The two of them were working together on a plain table and six chairs ordered by a gentleman for the kitchen in his new house at Ringwood in the New Forest. Fred yearned to progress further and to produce more elegant furniture, but he accepted that he now had a lifetime in which to achieve his ambitions. For the time being, he was very content. His more experienced workmates had just secured a valuable contract for fitting out a new ship at the docks in Southampton, and the mood in the workshop was justifiably upbeat and happy.

Four

As the days passed, Fred's sisters became very attached to Lucky. Even Fred's ma and pa seemed to accept the dog's presence without question, although Frederick still continued to warn, "That dog can't come to New Zealand with us, you know. What are you going to do about it?"

One hot summer day in July, Frederick returned home one evening in a great state of jubilation, announcing that he had booked passage for the family on the SS *Avalanche*, leaving Southampton on 11 September bound for Wellington. "It's only steerage," he admitted. "I can't afford any better accommodation, but I'm sure we will pass the time happily enough. The *Avalanche* is one of the fastest steamships in the world. She sails all that way to New Zealand in just over three months. Just think how wonderful it will be when we finally arrive in our new country. It will be the summer when we get there, and I'm quite sure I'll easily find employment, if not with the railway, then in some trade or other. Fred here, being a qualified carpenter, will have no trouble at all getting a job."

Fred had been listening to his father with growing dismay, knowing that the time had inevitably arrived when he would have to confess that he had no intention of going to New Zealand with the rest of the family. His pa was very excited, and Fred hated the fact that he was about to burst his bubble, but it had to be done—and right now.

"Pa," he said urgently, "please listen to me. I have something important to say, and I'm more sorry than I can say that it's going to upset you."

Frederick paused long enough to give his son an enquiring look before speaking. "I'm sorry about the dog, son, but I did warn you at the beginning that he would have to go eventually."

"That's just the point, Pa," Fred blurted out. "You see, I've decided I'm not coming with you. I'm going to stay here in England. I have a good job with many possibilities of promotion, so why should I risk it all by going off to the other side of the world? And of course, as you've mentioned, there is Lucky to consider. I love that dog. He trusted me to look after him, and I can't let him down now."

Frederick received his son's bombshell in an unusually quiet manner. Instead of arguing with him, he slowly smiled and said, "I'm not going to cancel your booking, my boy. When you have thought it through, I'm sure you will change your mind. How can you not be excited at the prospect of a new life in a new land?"

Fred wisely decided to let the matter drop for the time being, which would give his father the opportunity to assimilate the momentous decision he had made. He knew without any doubt that he would indeed stay in England and hoped that his father would eventually accept that fact.

Fred had not dared to look at his mother during this exchange. He understood that she would be extremely distressed at the thought of being separated from her only son, and it troubled him greatly to think of the hurt he was causing her. He was very surprised, therefore, when she quietly took him aside and said, "I can't help but agree with you, my dear boy. At present, your father is full of enthusiasm and genuinely wants the best for all of us, and consequently he is deaf to all that you try to discuss with him. I confess I shall find it very hard if you stay here, but we can write to each other, and maybe one day you will be able to come visit." She added with a touch of irony, "But tell me, if it hadn't been for Lucky, would you be sailing off with us on the *Avalanche*?"

"I honestly can't answer your question, Ma," Fred replied. "I may have been swayed by Pa's eagerness to build a prosperous life for us all, but I would still be very unwilling to leave behind all that I hold so dear in this country."

The days seemed to flash by with July and August gone in the twinkling of an eye. With the coming of September, Frederick at last accepted the fact that his son was not emigrating with them, although he couldn't resist making one more attempt to change his mind. One evening after their supper, he asked Fred to sit down with him to discuss the future.

"The rent on this house has been paid until the Michaelmas quarter day," he advised, "so you can stay here until the twenty-ninth of September. After that, however, you will have to fend for yourself. How will you manage? You don't earn enough money to rent your own rooms, and if you are still so set on keeping Lucky, you will find that lodgings could be difficult to come by. I am truly sorry that I can't give you some money to help, but every last penny I had was taken by our fares to New Zealand and the rent on a couple of rooms for when we eventually arrive."

Fred listened in silence, not willing to admit to his father that he had been fretting about this very issue. He knew that if he were to allow his misgivings to show, he might still find himself on board the *Avalanche*, and that would never do. Instead, he managed to say quite airily, "Don't worry about me, Pa. I've made plans. Everything will be all right." *Please,* he thought, *don't ask what those plans are, because to tell the truth, there are none.* He repeated, "Don't worry, Pa. Everything will be all right. But I will miss you all so much. And perhaps I should be asking you if you are quite sure about the tremendous step that you are about to take. I pray that you and Ma and the girls will be happy and fulfilled in your new lives. I know that my sisters regard this as a great adventure, but have you thought about their education and what they will do when they are grown up? How will you manage if you can't find a job?"

Frederick waved all these arguments aside with a flick of his hand. "New Zealand is not a land of savages, my boy. It may be thousands of miles away, but I understand the people are just like us. In fact, a great number of them are English, having taken the brave step to move out there long before the possibility entered my mind. It will be a wonderful experience. Don't you see that? We all hope that one day you will come to visit, but in the meantime we will write to you as often as we can, and maybe you will change your mind when you read about our exciting new lives."

"You never know," Fred said, "but for the time being, I prefer to take my chances here in England."

Five

No one in the Lee household slept a wink during the night of 10 September. Fred's four sisters, aged from six to twelve, were excited beyond measure by the thought of travelling such a long way in such a huge ship. Matilda, on the other hand, was filled with misgivings and the sorrow of leaving her friends and everything that was familiar and precious to her. Frederick was elated that the date of departure was at last upon them, whilst his son lay restlessly in his bed, questioning his decision to stay, worrying about his family and their tremendous undertaking, and also feeling a little fearful about his own future.

The family's scant belongings had been packed into a small trunk, and Frederick had hired a horse and cart to take them to the port of Southampton. It was arranged that Fred would return the horse and cart to the owner when he came home later.

The SS *Avalanche* had already left the East India Docks in London and was due to arrive in Southampton later that day. She was a fine three-masted iron clipper, only three years old, but the captain had already made the journey to Wellington a number of times and was considered a very competent and experienced master. On board there would be thirty-four crew members and sixty-three passengers, many of whom were returning to their homeland of New Zealand, whilst others, of course, were optimistic emigrants. Little did Frederick realise, when booking the family's passage, that travelling steerage was a most unpleasant affair. Everyone had a mattress to sleep on, and there were benches on which to sit during the day, but the atmosphere was dark, damp, and very smelly. It was here that cows and sheep were also housed—the cows for their milk, and the sheep to provide meat, as they were systematically slaughtered as the journey progressed. There were also chickens to supply eggs, and the constant noise they made could become unbearable. Frederick, having been informed by a rather supercilious clerk that steerage passengers were allowed to walk in certain areas of the deck at certain times of the day, hoped that this facility would help Matilda and her daughters cope with the severe restrictions otherwise imposed upon them.

At last dawn broke on the morning of 11 September 1877. Frederick was in a great state of excitement, bouncing around, issuing instructions, and constantly looking out for the arrival of the promised horse and cart. "Matilda!" he called out for the umpteenth time. "Have you got the passports and all the documents?"

"Yes, dear," Matilda somewhat wearily replied. "I have everything we need in my bag. Do try and calm down. You're worse than the girls." She gazed anxiously out the window, noting the heavy clouds and the rain beginning to spit down, and hoped the cart had a tarpaulin cover to provide them with shelter. "The weather's not good," she remarked. "I hope it clears up before the ship sails tonight, for otherwise the sea could be quite rough." Trying to put a smile on her face, she added, "Well, there's nothing we can do about the weather, so I suggest you all come to the table for our final meal together in our little cottage." She choked on her words and brushed away the tears that were threatening to fall. "I wonder what sort of breakfast they will give us on the ship. Porridge, no doubt, but probably not as tasty as mine."

At last their humble transport arrived at the door, and it seemed that the whole village had turned out to wish the family farewell. Matilda found herself surrounded by her friends, all intent on giving her a last hug, whilst Frederick endured many hearty slaps on the back. "Write to us, won't you? Let us know all about New Zealand. We'll take care of Fred—make sure he doesn't get into any trouble."

The last remark was accompanied by a wink in Fred's direction, but he felt too dispirited to comment.

Their journey to the docks took a little less than two hours. Matilda was thankful that there was indeed a tarpaulin cover to shield them from the rain, which was now pelting down. Very little was said during that two hours, each of them lost in their own thoughts. Even the sisters had ceased their chatter and were beginning to look cold and pinched. Lucky could sense that something momentous was happening and went around the whole family giving them consoling licks, all the time looking anxiously at Fred, who was surprisingly unresponsive towards him.

"There she is!" exclaimed Frederick when at last they arrived at the port. "What a splendid ship! Look over there; people are already boarding. I can't believe the quantity of luggage being taken up the gangway." Matilda looked at the small trunk which contained the clothes and effects for her entire family, and once again she shook her head at the enormity of what lay ahead for them. "Come along!" commanded Frederick. "I believe we have to go through the emigration process at that building over there." He turned to his son and, in an unusual display of affection, hugged him tightly. "Well, this is it, my boy. You can't come any further, so we had best say our goodbyes now."

I must not cry in front of Ma and the girls, Fred sternly admonished himself. *Just put a smile on your face and promise to write every week.* He hugged each of them in turn and then, finding it too difficult to speak, moved away from the little group as they made their way towards the port offices.

Matilda also found she could not speak. She had wanted to say so much to her son, to tell him how much she loved him, to wish him success in his career, to say she hoped he would be happy, but her voice failed and all she could do was kiss his dear cheeks and try to imprint his beloved face on her memory for all time. In the small trunk containing the family's belongings, she had included one precious photograph of Fred with Lucky by his side, having vowed this would take pride of place in their new home, wherever that might be. Frederick, too, found it difficult to say goodbye, but he was so fired up with enthusiasm and so keen to get started on his "great adventure" that the poignant moment of farewell passed almost without recognition.

The necessary proceedings prior to their embarkation seemed to take hours with passports and papers having to be checked by a number of rather bored-looking officials, who also annoyed Frederick by asking what he thought to be endless and quite unnecessary questions. Finally, however, the family emerged from the building to take the short walk towards the *Avalanche*, which was to be their home for the next three months. Fred had waited near the quayside in the hope that he might have one final glimpse of his family, but by now the rain was pouring down and the wind was gusting heavily. Although he waved to everyone approaching the ship, he could not be sure that it was them or, indeed, that they were aware of him. Nevertheless, he was determined to stay until the ship had sailed out of sight.

Six

In the meantime the remaining members of the Lee family had boarded the great ship. Once again their passports and all relevant papers were inspected by a kindly officer who gave Matilda a sympathetic nod of the head as he directed them to the steerage deck. Not knowing what to expect, Matilda was appalled at the scene which greeted her. There were about twenty other travellers who had arrived earlier, and the atmosphere was already claustrophobic, stuffy, and smelly. She burst into loud sobs. "Oh, Frederick! We can't live like this for the next twelve weeks. I thought we would have at least a small cabin for the six of us." Frederick tried to console her by putting his arm around her shoulders and muttering something about making friends with the other travellers to pass the time, about how they would probably get used to the conditions, and about how eventually, when they were settled in their new home, they would laugh about the whole experience.

Matilda would have none of it, her anguish suddenly giving way to a bout of fury. She violently pushed her husband away and shouted, "I will never forgive you for this! You have misled us! How could you?" She turned to her daughters, who were staring open-mouthed at her uncharacteristic anger, and said, "My darlings, I am so sorry. We will have to be very brave and put up with these conditions, but it will come to an end. And when we reach New Zealand, it will be summertime, so you can go out and breathe in God's good air." Then, putting her hand on Frederick's arm, she apologised for her outburst, saying, "I don't suppose you knew about this either, did you, my dear? I'm sorry I lost my temper. We must make the best of it now, but I shall be so very thankful when the next twelve weeks are over." Frederick nodded his agreement and kissed her cheek with some relief.

Matilda was somewhat appeased when dinner was served as it was a very tasty vegetable broth with chunks of bread, followed by, of all things, a banana. Annie had taken a bite and wrinkled up her nose in disgust until Matilda showed her how to peel off the skin and eat the delicious fruit inside. She herself had only ever heard of this exotic fruit as it was far too expensive for her household purse. By the time the meal was finished, the *Avalanche* had made her way down the Southampton waters and out into the ocean. She began to roll back and forth in the worsening weather, and the noise of the crashing waves drowned out any conversation that the family might have shared. Very soon most of the passengers, be they steerage or upper deck, were feeling extremely queasy and distressed.

"Oh, Ma!" cried out Edith in a very wobbly voice. "I don't like this. I feel sick, and I'm very frightened."

With a white face and a churning stomach, Matilda tried to comfort her children, suggesting they should lie down on their mattresses and hold hands. "This storm will soon blow itself out, and tomorrow when we have our allotted time on the deck, we can enjoy a stroll in the fresh air and smell the wonderful salty scent of the ocean."

Frederick boasted that he seemed to have found his sea legs already and that he didn't feel at all nauseous. In fact, he laughed his big booming laugh and declared, "What an adventure this is!" His fellow travellers glared at him in disbelief, and one or two muttered curses under their breath.

Back onshore, Fred stood on the quayside watching as the great ship slipped away from her moorings. He waved until he could see no more, and then with a heavy heart he went to collect the horse and cart and begin his solitary journey home. Lucky looked up at him with adoration as if to say he understood his master's sadness and would do his best to make him happy again. The rain was still pouring down, but Fred found that the tarpaulin kept him quite cosy. It had been a long day filled with great emotion, and now he just felt tired to his very bones and was longing to tumble into his bed. Two hours later, he pushed open the front door of his little home and inevitably was greeted by an eerie silence. Tears threatened again, but he brushed them away and went in search of the bread and meat which his mother had thoughtfully left for him and Lucky. After a couple of bites, however, fatigue overcame him and he fell fast asleep in his chair.

At some time in the night, Fred awoke with a violent start and a strange sense of foreboding, which he dismissed as the product of the emotional day he had endured. He shed his still damp clothes, climbed into bed, and once again fell fast asleep.

Seven

Some hours later, Fred was wakened by someone hammering on the door. “Fred! Fred! Are you in there? Open the door!”

Fred, rubbing his eyes and still half asleep, climbed out of bed, put his hand on Lucky’s back to stop his frantic barking, and called out, “Yes, I’m here. Whatever is the matter?”

He lifted the latch, and his neighbour Bert rushed in, waving a newspaper and exclaiming, “You can’t have seen this yet. Oh, you poor boy. However are you going to be able to cope? You will have to be very brave.”

Extremely alarmed by now, Fred held up his hand and demanded, “What has happened? Tell me!” A newspaper was thrust into his hands.

“Read that.” In big black headlines, the *Times* newspaper of that day screamed out, Two ships in collision off Portland Bill. No survivors.

Fred sank into a chair with his head in his hands and asked in a trembling voice, “Was it the *Avalanche*?”

“Yes,” Bert replied. “The other ship was the *Forest*, on its way to the United States. The storm was at its height, visibility was practically nonexistent, and the *Avalanche* was struck amidships, sinking in just a few minutes. I’m desperately sorry for you, lad. Would you like to come over to our house for a while?” Fred looked at Bert. For a moment, he felt too dazed to speak.

“Not just now, thank you,” he eventually replied with his voice breaking. “I have to take it all in first. It’s hard to believe that such a catastrophe has happened. It's kind of you to ask me. I'll come later. For now I'd like to be alone."

"Of course," Bert responded. "You just come along whenever you feel you want to talk or to have something to eat. I'll go now, but I'll leave the newspaper for you to read if you want." Bert felt he wanted to hug this devastated young neighbour of his, but he was not sure how such a gesture would be received, so he made a rather awkward departure.

Fred stayed in the chair, blankly staring at the walls. He felt numb, devoid of any emotion, and wondered if that was normal. Surely he should be screaming and shouting and sobbing his heart out. He picked up the newspaper and immediately threw it down. What was the point of reading it now? This unbelievably dreadful event had taken place and he would never see his family again. He had not been aware, of course, of the dire conditions imposed on steerage passengers, but he knew that his family would be on the lowest deck and therefore would have drowned almost immediately. He hoped they had all been asleep at the time of the collision and that his little sisters, in particular, had not been terrified by the fate awaiting them. They had been so excited. Fred found himself smiling sadly as he remembered their innocent prattle.

As the day slowly passed, Fred went through many complex emotions. From his initial numbness and refusal to believe the awful truth, he moved on to anger, and finally to overwhelming grief. He sobbed until there were no tears left. Lucky patiently sat by his side, watching him closely and occasionally giving him a lick. Fred roused himself to give Lucky his dinner, but for himself he could eat nothing. He was aware of his neighbours coming to the door to sympathise and to offer food and help, but he could not bring himself to acknowledge them. He guessed that his boss knew about the disaster and would not have expected him to go in to work, but tomorrow he would have to make the effort and face his fellow employees. By nightfall he found himself so emotionally exhausted that when he fell into his bed, he managed to sleep fitfully for a few hours.

The sleep did him some good. When dawn broke, Fred felt more composed and able to face the world. He had a bracing wash in cold water, donned some fresh clothes, and managed to eat a slice of bread for his breakfast before setting off for his place of work. The dreadful storm had long blown itself out, and the day was a typically mellow autumn day with the leaves just beginning to turn colour. In the mistiness of early morning, Fred trudged along with his head bent down, barely acknowledging the occasional greetings from fellow walkers, until he finally entered the familiar workshop and discovered a very muted atmosphere. He realised immediately with a sense of relief that his colleagues already knew about the tragedy and that he wouldn't have to explain his sombre demeanour to them. An awkward silence prevailed until his boss said, "It's brave of you to come in today, lad. We are all desperately sorry about what happened. If you want to talk about it, of course we're prepared to listen, but we won't mention it again if that's what you'd prefer."

"Thank you, sir," replied Fred. "I'd rather not talk about it. Yesterday was a terrible day for me, but I'm slowly coming to terms with what happened. I just want to try and get on with my life now."

His boss nodded, saying, "Right then, lad. Why don't you pick up your tools and finish the job you were doing last week?" He looked down at Lucky, who was already fast asleep on the workshop floor, and said with a smile, "I don't think your dog will be any trouble today. He's certainly not up to chasing my cat."

The following Sunday, the vicar of the local church held a memorial service to honour the deceased Lee family. It seemed that the whole village attended. Fred felt it was his duty to be there too, but inwardly he was raging at the cruel God who had dealt him such an unimaginable blow. *How can I sing God's praises?* he angrily questioned himself. *How can I listen to Reverend Potts praying for my family's eternal redemption and droning on about God's will?*

"There is no God," Fred announced to himself. "I will never believe again." Little by little, however, his neighbours' genuine warmth and compassion towards him began to melt the ice in his heart, and as he left the church, he managed to smile at the vicar and thank him for the trouble he had taken.

"It was no trouble," the vicar replied. "And please, Fred, you know you can talk to me at any time."

Fred nodded and quickly walked away, vowing that he would never enter the church again or ask for spiritual help.

Eight

Fred somehow got through the days. He worked automatically, exchanging very little conversation with his workmates, who seemed horribly embarrassed, not knowing how to approach him or what to say. They managed a perfunctory "Bye, see you tomorrow" at the end of the day, and Fred gave them a wave of his hand before trudging wearily back home with his head bent and his shoulders sagging. *Home,* he thought sadly. *It's not a home any more. It's just somewhere I eat and sleep, and even that won't be for much longer.* He was too mentally exhausted to consider the looming problem of where he was going to live. Lucky, always aware of Fred's emotions, walked quietly by his side with his big brown eyes constantly looking up to his master.

Every evening when Fred arrived back in his village, he was greeted by kindly neighbours, all anxious to do something to help. Some of them left food on his doorstep, which he very gratefully accepted as he knew he could not find the inner strength to prepare anything for himself. The little cottage somehow seemed desolate as though even the walls knew a tragedy had occurred. Although weariness burdened him, he found it difficult to sleep, and when he did manage to close his eyes, dreadful nightmares would assault him. He felt he was floundering in icy water and would wake up screaming, "I don't want to die!" His spirits were at their lowest, and he found himself wishing that he had indeed been on the *Avalanche* with his family and had suffered the same fate. He felt guilty that he had defied his pa in deciding to stay in England, and in doing so he was alive and well when all his loved ones were dead. The grim thought that he was now an orphan kept repeating in his head. He was on his own and was not yet twenty-one years old. Finally, he realised that his present way of thinking would only lead to grief and desolation, so he issued strict instructions to pull himself together. After all, he still had loving relatives not too far away. Poor Aunt Ann would be devastated by the news. He promised himself that he would visit her as soon as he could. Although he still felt very drained, his mood began to turn calmer, and one morning on his way to work the thought struck him that possibly, just possibly, his life had been saved for a purpose yet to be revealed. How intriguing!

Nine

Fred's boss noted with concern the black shadows under the eyes of his young employee and kindly asked him if he would like to take the day off. "That's very good of you, sir," replied Fred. "I'd rather keep working as usual, but when I do have a break, I will have to start looking for somewhere to live."

"Why is that?" his boss queried.

"Because the rent of my parents' cottage is only paid up until the twenty-ninth of September. I can't afford to stay there, and in any case, I don't want to go on living there now with that eerie silence all around. Sooner or later I'll have to make a fresh start."

His boss, Samuel Archibald Brown to give his full name, looked intently at Fred for a moment or two, then said, "I will see what I can do to help."

Fred took this to be a rather empty promise, but a few days later he was confounded when Samuel summoned him into his office and announced, "I have had a word with Mr Hyde, who, as you know, is one of our wealthier customers. I was aware that there are some disused stables on his property, which is about two miles from here. His wife used to ride, but she had an accident, you see. And although she is fully recovered, she has lost her enthusiasm. His daughters were never interested in riding, so the horses were eventually sold. The stables are sheltered and can easily be converted into a living space for you. What do you think?"

Fred took a moment or two to respond, so great was his relief. "I think that Mr Hyde is exceptionally kind. Thank you so much for asking him. I'd love to accept, but as you know, I can't afford much in rent. What would he be asking?"

"Well, that's it," Samuel replied, beaming. "Mr Hyde has said that as you will be living in the stables and preventing them from falling into disrepair, you will, in effect, be doing him a favour. Therefore, no rent will be required, although of course you will be responsible for your own upkeep and your dog's."

Fred could hardly believe his ears at this sudden turn of fortune. "Thank you so much, sir. I can't wait to move in and start making it a home for me and Lucky. You have taken a weight off my mind. I'm so very grateful."

"I'm just glad I was able to help. I will introduce you to Mr Hyde when he can spare the time, but in the meantime, of course, I've already given you a glowing reference." With this remark, Samuel patted Fred on the back. "It's good to see you smile again, young fellow. Don't forget, however, that it will take you a long time to come to terms with what has happened, so just take it one day at a time and eventually things will get easier for you." Fred felt tears beginning to spring up in his eyes, but this time they were tears of gratitude and relief that some of his worries were beginning to slip away.

The following week, Mr Hyde called in to see Samuel Brown, and Fred was able to personally express his profound gratitude for the generosity shown to him. For his part, Mr Hyde was quite taken with the young lad and happily acknowledged to himself that he had done the right thing in offering living accommodation, humble as it might be. His wife had been a little less accepting, bluntly stating, "If that young Fred casts eyes at our daughters, he will be out on his ear before he can turn round." Indeed, Mr Hyde had harboured similar thoughts because Fred was a good-looking chap. He promised himself he would issue a carefully worded warning when the opportunity arose. In the meantime, however, he could not help but smile at Fred's enthusiastic plans for his new quarters.

Ten

Ten days later, Mr Thompson, the landlord, arrived at the door of the family cottage to inspect the property and collect the key as Fred would be leaving that day. Mr Thompson was short and stout and had a pronounced limp, which he had sustained during his service in the Crimean War. In fact, it was the money he had received when he was invalided out of the army which had enabled him to invest in several properties to rent out to provide himself a decent living. He had always been honest and decent, even on one or two occasions "forgetting" to collect the rent when he knew his tenants were going through hard times.

Now, having made a thorough inspection of the cottage and finding it spotlessly clean and tidy, he turned to Fred and said, "Well, young fellow, I'm more sorry than I can say about the tragedy which has befallen your family, but in spite of your grief, you have kept the cottage clean and in good condition. Therefore, I am happy to return to you the deposit which your father paid when you all moved in here ten years ago."

"Deposit? What deposit?" Fred asked in astonishment.

"A full quarter's rent," Mr Thompson replied.

"And how much would that be?"

"With the interest incurred, it amounts to four pounds, ten shillings, and five pence."

Fred sat down into the nearest chair with a bump. "I had no idea," he said. "Pa just said he had paid the rent up to the end of this quarter.

He never mentioned a deposit. It seems an awful lot of money. Are you sure that's right?"

"Yes, it's right," replied Mr Thompson benignly. He put his hand on Fred's shoulder and continued, saying, "If I could give you some advice, young fellow, I would put the money in a reputable bank. That will keep it safe until you need it."

And so on 29 September 1877, Fred Lee finally closed the door of his family home and walked away towards his new life. *No tears. No looking back,* he sternly admonished himself. *I can't spend the rest of my life mourning the loss of my family. I will just remember the happy times here with Ma and Pa and the girls. That life had come to an end anyway with Pa's decision to emigrate. It's up to me now to prove that there must have been a reason for my salvation, and I shall do my best to find it.*

With Lucky by his side, Fred strode away towards his workplace with determination and a new, but very welcome, lightness of heart. He had only a few belongings, some pots and pans and one or two keepsakes, all of which he had placed into a small handcart which he now trundled along in front of him, thankfully acknowledging that the weather, although cool, was fine and dry.

Fred had always enjoyed the long daily walk, whatever the weather and in all seasons, even occasionally when the snow was deep and he slipped inside his sturdy boots, making his feet wet and cold. He loved the scent of the countryside in the spring and summer, the changing colours of the trees in autumn, and the tracery of their bare branches in winter. Now, he thought with some nostalgia, was the last time he would come this way, because Mr Hyde lived in the opposite direction in the village of Chilworth. Not only that, but also the road to Chilworth was fairly busy as it was near the main highway leading eventually to Winchester. Whilst some of his journey would take him along the banks of the river, a great deal of it would be through streets lined with all manner of dwellings, from large houses to quaint cottages and the occasional store. As he plodded along, he hoped that Lucky would adjust to all the changes. The dog did seem more confident nowadays, even though he was still reluctant to leave his master's side.

Although fully occupied with the task in hand, Fred found that his day seemed to pass very slowly. He was relieved when the time came round to knock off. It was already dark when he set off on the two-mile walk to his new home. In his handcart were a couple of meat pies which his kindly neighbour had provided, and he realised these and all his food for the next few days would have to be eaten cold until he could find the time to fix up some method of cooking and heating. He had also brought along two blankets and hoped there would be some straw left in the stables which he could use to fashion a makeshift mattress. On arrival, however, he found to his great pleasure that Mrs Hyde had left him a plate of bread and cheese and a tankard of beer. Not only that, but also standing in one of the stalls was a rather dilapidated bedframe with a deep mattress, and in another stall was a large armchair, which had definitely seen better days. *How kind!* Fred thought, sitting down in the surprisingly comfortable chair with a sigh of relief. "We seem to have fallen on our feet, don't we, Lucky?" Rousing himself again, he went outside to the yard to find the water barrel. Lucky thirstily lapped up a bowlful of water before sharing his young master's meal. Then, fully sated, he jumped up onto the bed and settled down for the night. Fred laughed out loud. "So, that's the way it's going to be, is it? You should really sleep on the floor, but I must admit this way we can keep each other warm." Within minutes, master and dog were sound asleep, only awaking hours later when the local cockerel began its morning cacophony.

As the days passed, Fred began to fall into a routine. He found it was easier to have his main meal of the day at work, where facilities were provided for cooking and heating. On his way back to the stables in the evening, he passed a small grocery, where he would stop to buy fruit, cheese, milk, tomatoes, and ham. On the whole, he felt very well provided for. He discovered a bank nearby and, having made a few enquiries about its stability and reputation, was happy to open up an account with them. *Just fancy that!* he thought with a smile. *Me, Fred Lee, a man of means!* It gave him a nice warm feeling inside to know that he could afford a few things to make his life more comfortable.

With that in mind, he bought a bedside rug and a thick eiderdown in readiness for the coming winter.

Fred saw very little of Mr and Mrs Hyde and nothing at all of their daughters, although he would occasionally hear the clatter of a horse and carriage and their laughter as they climbed aboard on their way to one of their leisurely pursuits. To be honest, he did not crave company and was aware in the recesses of his mind that the solitude of the stables and the regular routine of his days were all combining to heal his grief and help him come to terms with the tragedy. Occasionally he still suffered from bouts of irrational fury alongside the sadness, but again he understood that this was normal and sooner or later would pass. His former antagonism towards God and the church began to fade, and once again he could find comfort from his mother's wise teachings and her naïve but rock-solid beliefs. It also occurred to him that overnight he had become a man, no longer a lad with no responsibilities and plenty of time to spend with his friends. He felt he had long outgrown that period of his life and that those very companions would now seem tediously adolescent in their outlook.

Eleven

Samuel Brown and his wife, Deborah, were childless, a fact which had caused them a great deal of distress in their early marriage. Over the years, however, they had come to terms with the fact that they would never be blessed with children and had started to find many compensations, not least of which was being able to travel in their pony and trap to Southampton to visit the theatre, an art gallery, or one of the many friends they had made. The New Forest was also a favourite destination where they would admire nature's changes in each season and watch the wild ponies grazing. They were a sociable, kindly couple, devoted to each other. Samuel's only regret was that he had no son to whom he would pass on his business when the time came. An idea crossed his mind that Fred might indeed turn out to be a surrogate son. *But not yet,* his sensible self insisted. *Don't get ahead of yourself. Give Fred a few years to thoroughly learn the trade and see how the lad turns out before you do something you might come to regret.* For the time being he could see that Fred was hard-working and honest. He had dealt very bravely with the devastating blow he had received and had not allowed it to affect the quality of his work. In fact, Samuel was considering giving Fred more responsibility and a raise in his wages to six shillings a week.

The opportunity to give Fred more responsibility arose the very next week when an order came in for a table and eight chairs to be made for a local landowner's daughter who was getting married and setting up home just two miles away. On Thursday morning, Samuel called Fred into his office. "I want you to go over to this address and find out exactly what the young lady would like. I hear she has very definite ideas, so you will need to be tactful if you feel they're not quite right. I've just received a delivery of mahogany, so you might suggest that to her."

Ten minutes later a somewhat apprehensive Fred was on his way to his first big assignment, accompanied, as always, by his faithful friend Lucky. Samuel had already explained Fred's circumstances to his client, and she had readily given her permission for the dog to be present.

The day was cold but fine and dry. Fred tried to enjoy the short walk, but to tell the truth, he was knotted up inside. He need not have worried, because on arrival he was immediately put at ease by the bride-to-be and her mother. They invited him into the parlour and insisted he take some refreshment before they got down to the business of the day. Lucky behaved impeccably as usual, stretching out at Fred's feet and quietly remaining there until it was time to leave. Fred began to relax and was glad to note that his hands had stopped shaking and that when he spoke, his voice was clear and steady.

It seemed that in no time at all Fred was delighted to hear his customer saying, "Well, I think we have agreed on your design for my table and chairs, and I'm very happy that you have suggested mahogany. Everyone around here seems to use oak, and I really wanted something different. Now that you're here, I wonder if you could spare me a little more time to give me your ideas about a sideboard to match."

"Of course, madam," replied Fred, "and dare I suggest that you might also think about a small corner cupboard? Your dining room furniture suite would then be complete and will look really modern."

"You are a good salesman," replied his customer with a smile. "I like your ideas, but my father is financing all this, so I will have to ask him first. I'll let you know as soon as possible." Fred nodded in acceptance and then drew out his pad and pencil once again to start a rough draft of how he envisioned the sideboard might look. It was to be fairly plain but elegant with a scroll carved on the upstand to match those on the chairbacks.

After half an hour of concentration, Fred proffered his sketches to the young woman. "Yes," she said, "that is exactly what I had in mind. You're very clever to understand my vague descriptions so completely. Please, would you indulge me one further time and sketch your proposed corner cupboard? Then, when my father returns home, I can show him everything. Of course, we shall also need your price estimate. Would you like a cup of tea while you do your calculations?"

If Fred had any weak points, then this would count as one of them. His grasp of mathematics was rudimentary, and he understood very clearly that if he wanted to advance his career, he would have to address this weakness. However, for the present time, Mr Brown had given him some figures for the original order of table and chairs, so Fred merely doubled that price and trusted all would be well.

With the promise of a lucrative contract, Fred fairly bounced back to the works. He felt proud of himself and the good outcome he had achieved, but he told himself it would never do to become complacent or—and here he struggled to find the right word—vainglorious. He would also have to learn the art of estimating for a job as, without that skill, he could never move up the proverbial ladder. Also, this time his client had been a very pleasant person, but it was more than likely that in future he would have to deal with people less agreeable.

Samuel Brown was waiting in the office for Fred's return. A sense of relief swept through him when he saw his protégé striding towards the door with a beaming smile stretching from ear to ear. "I imagine it's good news," Samuel exclaimed.

Fred happily replied, "Yes, as you know the original commission was for a dining room table and chairs, but I think I've persuaded our client to add a sideboard and corner cupboard to her order."

"Very well done, lad. I had every faith in you. I trust you were very careful in your calculations before giving her a quotation?"

Fred nodded. "I hope so. In fact, I think I've erred on the side of asking a little too much, but the lady seemed happy enough."

"How long do we have to complete the order?"

"Until the spring, sir," Fred replied. "The lady is getting married in March and wants everything to be in place when she returns from her honeymoon sometime in April."

"That's entirely possible. The work will be done under the management of John Wilson, but I want you to be his right-hand man. You will gain more valuable experience in the process. In the meantime, I'm raising your wages to six shillings a week."

"Thank you very much, sir," Fred replied gratefully.

On his way back to the stables that evening, Fred thought back over the day and all that had happened. "Lucky," he said, looking down to address his dog, "we must celebrate. I think I'm finally on the way up the ladder." Unexpectedly, a wave of sadness swept over him as he realised there was nobody in his life now who could celebrate with him, except maybe his dear aunt Ann. His pa would undoubtedly have said a gruff "well done", whilst his ma would have clasped him to her not insubstantial bosom and kissed him enthusiastically on both cheeks. Even his sisters would have been pleased for him. Oh, how he missed them all! *Will I ever get used to being on my own?* he wondered. Shaking himself metaphorically, he forced the unhappy thoughts away and tried to concentrate on the present time.

Twelve

By this time it was late November, and the stables, which had seemed such a cosy refuge just two months ago, were now cold and rather inhospitable. *Come on,* Fred urged himself, *you can do better than this now. You have money in the bank and a raise in wages. Maybe it's time to move on.* This last thought came as somewhat of a surprise, but then he began to take it seriously. *Surely I can afford some proper lodgings now,* he pondered, *although having Lucky may prove to be a bit of a stumbling block. But there's no harm in making some enquiries.* Then he decided that actually it might be better to wait another month or so, when the Christmas and New Year festivities would be over and life would have settled back into its usual pattern.

Aunt Ann and Uncle William had asked Fred to join them for Christmas, with his aunt adding, "Lucky as well, of course, my dear." Despite their underlying sadness, they were determined to make it a cheerful, happy time, especially as their young family were becoming more and more excited as each day passed.

As their parents had done many years before, they followed the custom of hanging a different picture on the wall each day. Usually they produced their own drawings, but occasionally William would bring home a brightly coloured postcard. It was thanks to the newly introduced bank holiday that Fred would have three whole days to enjoy some leisure and, even more important, his aunt's delicious cooking. He tried to think of suitable presents for the family and finally had the brainwave of making individual wooden boxes for them. He planned a large but plain one for William, a smaller but more ornate one for Ann, and a box with a secret drawer for each of the three children. He asked Mr Brown if he could use the workshop after hours because it was warm in there and had better lighting. Permission was readily given, together with an offer to use up any off cuts that were available.

Fred realised he had given himself quite a task to get the work finished in time for Christmas, but he was determined to meet the deadline, so he often worked late into the night in addition to all the hours of his one occasional free day. At last the five boxes were finished to Fred's satisfaction and were wrapped up and stowed away in the little handcart into which he had also packed a change of clothes for his stay. On Christmas morning, he and Lucky set off. At some point along their journey, Lucky jumped into the handcart, settling down with a doggy grin on his face. Fred laughed out loud and paused to give his dog a pat on the back and a tickle under the chin, causing Lucky to wag his tail frantically. "My goodness!" Fred exclaimed. "You've got a nerve, but I wish I could climb in with you."

Aunt Ann greeted Fred with a warm hug and a kiss on each cheek, and once again he realised how much he missed the personal contact he had enjoyed with his own family. *Maybe one day I'll find a wife,* he thought, *and we will have children. That would be so good.* In the meantime, he was determined to enjoy the break in his regular routine, to be cheerful and happy, and to be good company to these dear people.

The three days passed all too quickly, and sooner than he would have wished Fred was on the road again, back to his humble stables and his lonely existence. This time, however, his mind was full of happy memories of the Christmas he had just spent. His gifts had been very well-received. Aunt Ann immediately found some trinkets to put in her box, whilst Uncle William declared he had always wanted somewhere safe to keep his pipe, his tobacco, and his beloved velvet smoking cap. Fred's small cousins were equally intrigued by their secret drawers, each one of which was different. As for Fred himself, he was very pleasantly surprised to receive a warm scarf knitted by his aunt, a terracotta pot made by his uncle, and various drawings of Christmas trees and snowmen from his cousins. Even Lucky had not been forgotten as Aunt Ann had knitted him a small blanket to keep his back warm during the winter.

Fred still felt slightly antagonistic towards the church and was disinclined to accompany the family when they went along to the Christmas service early in the morning. However, he walked with them to the church anyway, where they were greeted by their vicar. "Good morning to you all. Please come in." Fred shook his head, indicating Lucky as his excuse. However, he heard the response, "All God's creatures are welcome! Even if this one barks!"

It seemed as if the ice around Fred's heart began to melt as the service progressed. It was joyous and comforting, and he sang the familiar carols at the top of his voice. He remembered with a pang how he had once enjoyed singing and made a vow that he would try to sing again, even if he should be alone at the time.

Later that day, they all had sat down to an enormous dinner, which Aunt Ann had somehow cooked to perfection despite all the hubbub around her. Memories of that dinner now made Fred's mouth water. There had been a succulent goose with roast potatoes and vegetables from Uncle William's garden, followed by little pies filled with minced meat and a rich gravy. Dessert consisted mainly of a delicious figgy pudding cooked in accordance with Mrs Beeton's recipe, and afterwards there were all manner of sugar buns, cinnamon biscuits, and chunks of fudge. Fred's young cousins were much the same age as his own sisters would have been, and he had enjoyed keeping them amused with various games such as jacks, pick-up-sticks, tiddlywinks, and a new card game called "Happy Families", which had been one of their presents. There had even been a little Christmas tree in the corner of the room, laden with decorations and sweetmeats, and Fred remembered with a chuckle how Lucky had been caught stealing one of the latter.

There had been one further surprise for Fred. On the third and final day of his stay, a mysterious package lay by his plate when he arrived at the breakfast table. He looked at it and turned it over several times, but there were no clues. "Go on!" His aunt laughed. "Open it up!" Inside Fred discovered a fine leather wallet and a small card with the words "For your belated twenty-first birthday, 11 October 1877. With our love, Aunt Ann and Uncle William."

"Well, I never," said an astonished Fred. "Thank you so much for remembering. I almost forgot it myself, but then, of course, I wasn't in the mood for celebrating at the time." Once again a sharp pang of sadness hit him. How different the day would have been if his family had still been with him. Again he shook himself mentally, acknowledging that these bouts of melancholy were inevitable. But they would surely ease in time.

Thirteen

Fred made his way back to the stables, which seemed cold and harsh after his stay in his aunt and uncle's warm and comfortable cottage. *Yes,* he decided, *it is definitely time to move on.* He would have to approach Mr Hyde and tell him how much he appreciated his offer of accommodation when he had not known which way to turn, but now he was in a better frame of mind, and having a little money in the bank, he could think more positively about his future. Before he could approach his landlord, however, he was surprised one evening to find Mr Hyde waiting for him when he returned from work.

"Good evening, sir. Would you like to come in?"

"No, thank you," Mr Hyde replied. "This won't take long. I have something to tell you, and I'm so sorry if it's going to cause you trouble." Fred gave him an enquiring look, but before he could say anything, Mr Hyde continued. "The thing is … well, the thing is … I'm really sorry, but the thing is …" He finally managed to blurt out, "I've been offered a new position in London, and as it's a good promotion in my career, I have decided to accept. We shall be moving up there shortly. The house has already been sold. Unfortunately, the new owners are keen horse riders, so, naturally, they want to be able to use the stables. I am so worried for you, Fred. What will you do?"

Fred found it difficult to stop a smile from spreading across his face. He hastened to reassure his benefactor that in fact the news was the spur he needed to go find himself another home. "When are the new owners moving in?" he asked. A small niggling worry entered his mind when he was told it would be in four weeks' time. That didn't give him much time. He would have to start his enquiries immediately and keep his fingers crossed that something would come up before the end of January. Mr Hyde seemed very much relieved by Fred's assertion that in any case he had been thinking about moving in the spring. After a mutual exchange of good wishes for each other's future, they shook hands and parted.

Fourteen

"So that's that, Lucky!" Fred exclaimed as he watched Mr Hyde make his way across the yard and enter the side door of his house. "Let's hope we can find a landlord who will fall for your winning ways." The next day, Fred asked Mr Brown if he could leave work an hour early because he wanted to speak to the editor of the local newspaper about inserting an advertisement in that week's edition. Fred was optimistic that, despite the expense, a positive outcome could be achieved and hopefully he would have several options to choose from. With permission granted, he and Lucky set off towards the press office, which was situated in a large building about three miles away. Lucky had gained a great deal of confidence over the past few weeks, and although he didn't like the noise of the traffic or the general hubbub around him, it didn't terrify him as it once had. He walked quietly by Fred's side and waited patiently whilst Fred explained his situation to the newspaper staff.

The advertisement appeared the following Friday, and on that Saturday, Fred once again made his way to the press office in a fever of anticipation to see the response. He was appalled to discover that there had been absolutely nothing. "This is really serious, Lucky," he said. "I thought we would have a few replies, even if they were not suitable for us. But nothing …?" Realising how strange it must look to other people to be caught talking to a dog, he abruptly left the office, bitterly regretting the waste of his precious money.

Despite its being mid-January, the weather was mild and the winter sun shone from a cloudless sky. Fred decided to take a detour back to the stables, which would be about a couple of miles farther but through more pleasant surroundings. He had anticipated being out for most of the day, so he had brought along a bottle of cider, a large Cornish pasty which he would share with Lucky, and a rather wizened apple for himself. *Cheer up,* he admonished himself. *This is the first and only setback. I'm sure there will be plenty of opportunities in the next week or so.* He refused to admit to any negative thoughts and profoundly hoped that something would indeed turn up.

Later that day, Fred acknowledged that fate has a strange way of intervening in life. *What if?* he asked himself. *What if I had gone straight back to the stables? What if that kind woman had not stooped to give Lucky a pat on the back, and what if we had walked away without exchanging a word with her?* Be that as it may, when Dora Hancock, as she introduced herself, had stopped to greet Lucky, Fred had smiled at her and said, "He likes that. Now he will be your friend forever."

So began a conversation which led to Dora's being told all about Fred's current worries, to which she replied, "I have spare premises which I was planning to let out. It's a very small one-up, one-down cottage which my son and his wife lived in when they were first married. Now they have two children and have moved to a bigger place a few miles away, and my cottage is empty. I never thought I'd be offering it to a total stranger without asking for references, but somehow I know I can trust you. Would you be interested?"

Fred took a moment to reply, so overwhelmed was he by this unexpected, generous offer. He fought off tears of gratitude before recovering. With a huge smile on his face, he turned to Dora. "I can't begin to say how grateful I am. You must have been sent from the gods. And if it were not so impertinent, I would hug you! Are you sure about this? I can produce references, and I have a little money in the bank. How much rent would you be asking? Would you mind my dog being there as well?"

Dora held up her hand and laughingly replied, "One thing at a time, young man. You may not like the cottage, and it may be too far from your place of work. I presume you do have a job, don't you? Why don't you come back tomorrow? Bring your references if you wish, but I can trust my instinct that you won't let me down. In the meantime, I will discuss all the details with my son, and we can sort it out then." She laughed. "My son will probably think I've lost my mind, but I'm sure he will see my point of view when he meets you."

By the time Fred arrived back at the works, it was well past ten o'clock and the place was in darkness. He knew, however, that his boss would be there at first light despite its being a Sunday, so he left a short note explaining the turn of events and asking if he could possibly have a reference to show to Mrs Hancock. Sure enough, Samuel Brown was only too happy to oblige. He said to his young protégé, "Good luck, lad. You can tell me all about it tomorrow."

Once again, Fred set out on what was to become a very familiar path. Dora was waiting at the gate, and together they went into her cosy parlour, where a welcome drink was awaiting him. Lucky thirstily emptied a bowl of water before wagging his tail and licking Dora's hand to show his gratitude. "Look at him," exclaimed Fred. "Usually he is very shy around strangers, but he seems quite at ease with you." He went on to say, "I've brought the reference from my boss," then he handed over the sealed envelope to Dora.

She quickly scanned the contents and smiled at Fred. "It's just as I thought. Your boss obviously has a very high opinion of you, saying you are honest and hard-working. He also mentions how well you dealt with your tragic circumstances a few months ago. Would you like to tell me about that? Don't, if you would rather not."

Fred discovered rather to his surprise that he would very much like to tell his story to this kind woman. For the next half hour she listened intently, nodding occasionally and finally taking hold of his hand in a gesture of sympathy. "I'm sure you have had enough people telling you how sorry they are," she said. "I won't do that, but what I can do is to offer you my help and friendship and an ear to listen whenever you feel the need. Changing the subject, my dear, may I ask how old you are?"

Fred gave a rueful smile and said, "I turned twenty-one last October, but obviously I wasn't in the mood for celebrating, and the date more or less slipped by without my noticing."

"Give yourself time, Fred. It will get easier, I promise.

"Now, Fred, I'm sure you're eager to see the rooms I'm offering you. Did I mention that they are just next door? We haven't discussed the matter of rent yet, have we? Small premises such as the one I am offering you usually cost one shilling and six pence a week. Would you find that acceptable?" Fred nodded his agreement. He had hoped it would be slightly less, but he had to remember that Lucky might cause a little more wear and tear than if he had been living there on his own. In any case, he felt this opportunity was heaven-sent, and he wasn't going to let it get away from him.

Remembering that his pa had paid a deposit on their family home, Fred asked the question of Dora. "Oh, I don't think that will be necessary," she replied, "though perhaps we should ask my son. He will be along shortly." With a twinkle in her eyes, she added, "He doesn't know yet what I've been up to, but I sense that you and he will get on very well together despite his being ten years older than you."

Fifteen

Exactly one week later, Fred was once again on the road, pushing along his handcart, which was overflowing with clothes and blankets, pots and pans, and an assortment of personal bits and pieces. "No room for you this time, Lucky." He chuckled. "It will do you good to walk, and the exercise will keep you warm. It's really cold today, isn't it?" As usual, he spoke aloud to Lucky. The thought crossed his mind that he would really have to curb the habit. It was all well and good when he was on his own, but if Dora heard him chattering away, she might be inclined to think she had rented out to a madman—and that would never do. His thoughts led back to the week before when he had met Dora's son for the first time. Richard had approached him with his hand outstretched, and they had instantly formed a liking for one another, discovering also that they worked in similar trades as Richard was a plasterer. They joked that one day they might set up in business together. Dora reminded them that many a true word is spoken in jest.

Richard apologised for the fact that the little one-up, one-down house was bare of furniture as he and his wife had needed everything for their new home. Fred thought longingly of the comfortable bed he had been forced to leave behind at the stables and wondered if he could possibly find some means of transporting it over. But then he decided it would probably cost the same and be far less trouble if he were to just buy a new one. He promised himself he would see to that as soon as possible. *After all,* he thought with a touch of self-satisfaction, *I have money in the bank, and I can afford one or two luxuries, if indeed a bed can be termed a luxury.* In the meantime, the blankets he had with him would have to suffice, and he and Lucky could curl up together to keep warm. He had noted to his relief that the little house seemed to be remarkably draught-free, which was a blessing, and there was enough wood to keep a fire burning for at least a couple of weeks.

It was thus with a great spirit of optimism that Fred arrived at No. 7 Rose Crescent, Toot Hill, which, although he did not know it at the time, was to be become his home for the next ten years. It was a new beginning for him, and he felt in a strange way that the twenty-one years he had already lived through now belonged to the past. This was where the rest of his life would start.

Dora and Richard were both at the door to greet him as he arrived. They spent the next hour or so making sure his meagre possessions were all put in place and that he was as comfortable as possible. "Have you eaten anything today?" Dora asked. Fred realised that indeed he was very hungry. He had been so preoccupied that, apart from a crust of bread and an apple at breakfast, the day had passed without his taking in any food. He shook his head and was about to say, *I'm all right, thank you. I'll find something,* when Dora took him firmly by the arm and said, "Come with me. I have a nice beef stew which has been cooking all day, and there is plenty for the three of us. Lucky can eat up the leftovers when we have finished." Fred was so overwhelmed with gratitude that he could only nod his acceptance.

An hour later, an enormous yawn overtook Fred, and he excused himself from the table to make his way back to No. 7. Once there, he wrapped several blankets around himself and fell instantly asleep, only rousing some hours later when Lucky gently licked his face and gave a little bark as if to tell his master that a new day was about to begin.

Sixteen

As soon as he had some time off work, Fred made his way into town to withdraw some money from his bank account with the intention of buying a new bed. Having successfully negotiated all the necessary form filling and the identification process, he strolled across to the local shopping thoroughfare, where he was surprised to find several shops, each offering a large selection of furniture. He browsed for some time before finally choosing a rather splendid affair with a metal frame, brass knobs at each corner, and one of the newly invented coiled spring mattresses. Fred was concerned that it might not be possible to lift the frame up his narrow winding staircase, but the helpful salesman pointed out that it could easily be taken to pieces and put together again when in position. He also suggested that the deliverymen would do the job for him for a small tip. So the deal was done, and Fred parted with far more than a week's wages for his new acquisition. He did have a fleeting moment of doubt but then sensibly decided that it was a very good investment.

Feeling rather pleased with himself, Fred hummed a tune as he left the shop, fully intending to return to No. 7 without delay. However, as he walked along the main street, he noticed how many people were riding bicycles. In fact, they outnumbered all those on horseback. A germ of an idea began to play in his mind. On a whim, he turned back in search of a shop selling these amazing contraptions. Half an hour later he could not believe what he had just done. He had actually bought a bicycle! It had been easy to persuade himself that it would be invaluable for travelling to his workplace and also for the occasional jaunt into the countryside or down to the coast. Admittedly, it was a rather uncomfortable ride as he bumped along on its solid rubber tyres. And he fell off several times before he got the hang of balancing on two wheels. However, he thoroughly enjoyed the feeling of freedom as he careered down the hills with the wind blowing through his hair. He realised with a grin that it was the first nonessential purchase he had ever made, and it was a good feeling to know that he could afford it. Lucky seemed content to bound along beside him, pausing only for a drink of water or an investigative sniff along the roadside.

Lately the dog had formed an attachment to Dora, and sometimes when the weather was wet and cold, he was content to stay with her during the day, curled up on one of her easy chairs. Fred was concerned that he was taking a liberty, but Dora assured him that she enjoyed the dog's company. Now that he had his bicycle, the journey to work was accomplished in a much shorter time, and Fred's energy seemed unstoppable. He worked very hard, gaining more and more experience with each day that passed. He managed to secure another contract on the recommendation of his first client, and this time the order was for a complete bedroom suite. Fred looked forward to it taking shape under the skilled hands of him and his fellow workers. From then on the orders came in regularly. Some were quite complicated, whilst others were just small commissions, but as Samuel Brown happily pointed out, "'Tis all grist t' the mill, lad."

Seventeen

Over the next five years, Fred led a contented life in his little cottage. He was amused to note how much attention Lucky attracted when he was out and about with him. Many comments were made: "What a good dog!" "How did you train him to be so obedient?" and "You can see he adores you." Fred found himself telling the story over and over again of how Lucky had come to be with him. He did not usually share the full details of the *Avalanche* tragedy, but in the way of small villages, the full tale eventually became common knowledge. Good solid friendships were made, and whenever Fred felt he could do with some company, he would make his way to the local pub and enjoy a pint of ale with his mates. He sometimes played skittles, but he much preferred darts, finding to his surprise that he had a good eye for the game. More often, however, he could be found in the snug with the other men, exchanging news and views with gusto, whether the topics were light and jokey or more weighty, such as the election of William Gladstone as prime minister or the fact that primary education for children was now compulsory. Even though Fred had no children, of course he held definite opinions and would debate the issue at some length. Having had the benefit of a good basic education himself, he was firmly in favour, but found to his surprise that some of the men did not agree with his views. Whenever he strolled down the lane leading to the pub, he thought how appropriate it was to be called "the Carpenters Arms", but the brightly coloured sign hanging from a bracket outside and showing a well-muscled chap wielding a large saw was a little too fanciful for his tastes.

In 1883 two major events occurred which rocked Fred's rather humdrum existence. On the first of January, his boss called him into the office. "Nothing to worry about, son," he said. "I just want to discuss a few plans that I have in mind. Sit down there and I will tell you." A few moments later, an intrigued Fred was astounded to learn that Samuel Brown was planning to retire. Not only that, but also he wanted to promote Fred so that in the very near future he would be in charge of the whole company. "I've watched you over the years," he said, "and I've every confidence that I'll be leaving the company in good hands."

Fred stammered his thanks, saying, "I had no idea that you had this in mind for me. I'm very flattered, to say the least, and I will do my very best to run the company as successfully as you have done. Your decision has left me quite dumbfounded. I really don't know what to say. 'Thank you' seems totally inadequate." With a slight frown, he added, "How do the other men feel about this? After all, most of them are older than me."

"They are all good workers," his boss replied, "but you have the necessary flair for understanding our customers' requirements, for designing exactly what they want, and for making sure that our company produces first-class workmanship." For a moment Fred felt an apprehensive chill. What if he didn't live up to Mr Brown's confident expectations and the company began to fail? It was a heavy responsibility. Was he up to the challenge? Seconds later, however, elation swept over him and his optimism returned. Of course, he could do it!

It seemed that Mr Brown was in no immediate hurry to retire, but he promised that come the spring he would be gone. In the meantime, Fred was busy learning the managerial ropes. It was then that the second event took place. Dora fell ill with what she described as a heavy cold, but this developed into pneumonia, and it seemed that in no time at all she had passed away. Fred grieved for this kind and generous woman who had played such a significant part in improving his life. Her death brought back all the sadness he had felt when he had lost his own family, and an air of utter despondency settled upon him. It seemed that everyone he held dear was being taken from him. Lucky looked at him with his big brown eyes, almost as if he understood the turmoil his beloved master was experiencing. He licked Fred's hand, and Fred turned to him, suddenly weeping uncontrollably into the dog's patient neck. Some time later when his sobs had subsided, he realised that in the years since his family had perished, he had never lost control of himself in such a way. He felt exhausted but strangely peaceful; it had been a truly cathartic release in many ways.

Dora's son, Richard, dealt with his own grief by launching into the business of tidying up his mother's affairs as soon as possible. It irked him that the solicitor he had employed seemed to take an inordinately long time to sort out the legal side, and he grumbled all the time about the unfortunate fellow. Fred, understanding that this was a sort of defence mechanism, wished he could help as Richard had become a good friend over the years that they had known one another. His opportunity came one Saturday evening when he had just returned home from work and found Richard in the front garden struggling to manhandle a large armchair up the path and through the front door.

"Here. Let me help you," Fred said, and together they manoeuvred the chair into position in the parlour, where its pair was already installed.

Laughing, the two men collapsed into the seats, with Richard exclaiming, "I think we deserve a drink, don't you? Let's go down to the Carpenters Arms."

They strolled companionably down the lane with the faithful Lucky at their heels and were fortunate to find a table in a quiet corner away from the noisy bar. Fred, thinking this would be a good opportunity to allow his friend to express his feelings, tentatively broached the subject of Dora's death. "You don't have to talk about it if you don't want to," he said sympathetically, "but I know what it's like to lose someone you love, and I'm happy to listen."

Richard proceeded to unburden himself at great length. When an hour had passed, he suddenly paused and said, "Do you know, Fred, I feel so much better now. Thank you for listening."

It transpired from their chat that Richard was intending to move into his mother's home with his wife and two children. "We certainly need the space," he said, "and it'll be grand living back in the village again with you as our neighbour." Fred listened to this with a sense of relief as a niggling worry had settled in his mind that the situation was different now and Richard might have other plans for his small abode. However, he was not prepared for the bombshell that Richard was about to deliver.

"I've been wanting to tell you something important," Richard said, "but I've been waiting for that tardy solicitor of mine to make it official. However, this is as good an opportunity as we'll get." He paused for a second. "I'm sure you know my mother thought very highly of you." Fred acknowledged the fact with a nod of his head, wondering where all this was leading. "Well," Richard went on to say, "you may be surprised to learn that she has left you the cottage in her will. Lock, stock, and barrel, it's yours!"

Fred stared at his friend, barely able to take in what he was saying. For the second time in just a few weeks, he found himself short of words to express his gratitude. "I just can't believe it! Oh, I do wish I could thank her in person. It's such a generous thing for her to have done. Just think, me, Fred Lee, a homeowner and still in my twenties! My ma and pa would never have believed it. I've been shown so much kindness and generosity in the years since I lost them, and I truly feel that it's up to me now to achieve the best that I can in their memory."

Eighteen

Now that he was in a much stronger frame of mind, Fred decided that he wanted to learn more about the night of 11 September 1877, the terrible storm, and the sinking of the SS *Avalanche*. He resolved that when he had time, he would find a library and look up the newspaper reports. The opportunity arose a couple of weeks later, and he made his way into town, leaving Lucky alone in the cottage. The dog was beginning to show his age now and was quite happy to stay at home, cosy and warm in a chair, until his master returned.

Having parked his bicycle and secured it with a strong padlock, Fred climbed the steps to the library and opened the door. He was greeted by a pleasant young woman, who asked if she could help him. "Yes, thank you," he replied. "I'd like to see copies of the *Dorset Echo* from September 1877."

"Certainly, sir." She smiled at him. "Please take a seat, and I will bring you everything you need." Fred was quite surprised that she hadn't asked any questions, but he was also relieved that he wouldn't have to explain his request. He was soon settled at the table with the relevant newspapers spread out in front of him. With mixed feelings of anticipation and dread, he began to turn the pages.

He remembered his pa telling him that the SS *Avalanche* was a three-masted iron sailing ship which had already made the long voyage to New Zealand three times under the experienced captain E. Williams. That fateful day, there were sixty-three passengers and thirty-four crew on board. Fred soon realised that living conditions for his family would have been utterly dreadful. His heart went out to his ma, who had so selflessly bowed to her husband's wish to emigrate. She had loved her little home in England, was happy and contented with her life and her many good friends, and yet she had agreed to give it all up. Fred could only guess at her despair when confronted with the reality of steerage accommodation and the thought that this would have to be endured for three long months.

He went on to read about the terrible storm which had engulfed the coast that dreadful night and how, fifteen miles off Portland Bill, the *Avalanche* had been rammed by another ship called the SS *Forest*, which had been making her way to New York with twenty-two crewmen aboard. The passenger ship had sunk within five minutes, whilst the *Forest* lasted an hour and a half before succumbing to the waves, with only a handful of the crew managing to escape.

Deeply engrossed in this tale of tragedy, Fred was unaware that the librarian had been looking in his direction with some concern. "Are you all right, sir?" she asked. "Only you seem a little distressed. Would you like a drink?"

"Thank you, but no," replied Fred, rather embarrassed that she had heard his occasional groan whilst he had been reading all the reports. He smiled across the room at her but decided that now was not the time to tell her his story. Instead, he turned back to the newspapers and continued to read. He learned of the bravery of the local men who had taken to the dangerously rough seas in their small rowing boats called lerrets in an effort to save lives. Three crewmen from the *Avalanche* had apparently tried to scramble across to the *Forest*, only to drown when their small boat capsized in the mountainous waves, but twelve men from the *Forest* had indeed been rescued, including their captain, William Lockhart.

A public subscription had been set up in memory of all those lost, and money had poured in from all over the world, particularly Australia, New Zealand, and of course Great Britain. In no time at all the enormous sum of two thousand pounds had been raised, and it was immediately agreed that all fourteen of the valiant sailors who had set off from Chesil Point in the rescue bid should receive ten pounds each. The remainder of the money was to be used to build a memorial church at Southwell, overlooking the area where the disastrous accident had occurred. On reading this, Fred was a little surprised that he had not been approached for a donation, but then he realised that, of course, he had moved a couple of times and had not left a forwarding address on either occasion. He vowed, however, that he would visit the church as soon as he had the time, and maybe he would be able to add his own personal memento. He thought vaguely of an embroidered hassock, or a painting, or an illustrated book perhaps. Apparently at the first service held in the little church, a candle which had been washed ashore from the wreck was lit. Fred thought how this gesture must have produced many poignant emotions among the congregation.

By this time, Fred was beginning to feel rather hungry. Realising he had been poring over all the records for the best part of three hours, he rose rather stiffly to his feet, smiled across at the librarian, and thanked her for her help. He could tell she was eager to hear his story, but he couldn't bring himself to relive it all over again for the time being. Maybe he would return one day, but for now he just wanted to go home, have something to eat, and enjoy Lucky's soothing company.

Nineteen

On a Monday morning some two months later, Fred set off for work as usual. It was a cool but sunny day. He whistled cheerfully as he cycled along. Lucky seemed to pick up on his mood, trotting alongside his master with his tail high and his eyes bright, occasionally veering off to investigate something of doggy interest, but always bounding back before Fred got too far ahead. As they entered the yard, Fred nearly fell off his bicycle in astonishment, as overnight a new sign had been erected. It announced in big bold letters:

BROWN & LEE
MASTER CARPENTERS
QUALITY FURNITURE MAKERS

Fred could hardly believe his eyes. With a mixture of emotions—pride at his achievement and sadness that his ma and pa were not there to congratulate him—he pushed open the door and entered. He was met by a hearty cheer from all his workmates, whilst Samuel Brown clapped him on the back, saying, "That surprised you, didn't it, lad?" Fred could only nod in agreement. "Come into the office with me," his boss continued. "There are one or two matters I want to discuss with you and, of course, a few forms to complete to make it all legal. My solicitor will be arriving shortly to see to all that. When everything has been signed and sealed, my wife and I plan to travel, first to London and then around the country, so you will be in charge. I hope you are happy about everything."

"It's a huge responsibility," replied Fred, "but I'll do my very best for the company. The men on the payroll are a great bunch of workers, and with their help I'm sure we will succeed."

Samuel Brown had always been a forward-thinking boss, and for some time his staff had been given not only every Sunday off work but also an extra day once a month of their choosing, all fully paid. They also benefitted from the newly introduced bank holidays and, of course, Easter and Christmas. This made Samuel Brown a popular employer, much to the chagrin of other bosses in the area who were not so generous. Fred intended, of course, to follow the same course of action, but he was also toying with the revolutionary idea of closing the works for one whole week every summer. He decided to keep this plan to himself for the time being to make sure that the company finances could support such a scheme.

Fred was young and energetic and brimming with ideas for the future. He hoped one day to expand the business and perhaps merge with a building company because there would be plenty of work available in Southampton. The docks and the railways had attracted a huge number of people to the area in recent years, and he was quite sure there would be a market for the type of houses he had in mind. He had to keep reminding himself, however, that Rome wasn't built in a day and that he should keep a cool head and slow down a little, but his enthusiasm was infectious, and his men responded in like manner.

Word soon spread that old Samuel Brown had retired and that some new chap, Fred—or was it Frank?—had taken his place as head of the company. Orders were a little slow coming in for a while, but Fred was astute enough to realise that people could be wary. Although he had been with the company for some time, he still had to prove himself as the boss. He decided to take out an advertisement in the local paper and cycled into town one day to place his order. Something, he thought, along the lines of, "Under new management, but still the same enthusiastic, hard-working, and skilled workforce.

We are a dedicated team and take pride in everything we make." He confidently parted with the shilling that it cost to advertise, and in the coming weeks his optimism was rewarded when the company received a large number of enquiries and positive orders.

On the day of Fred's trip into town, he decided to visit the library again to further his acquaintance with the young woman who had seemed so sympathetic on his previous visit. To his great disappointment, however, there was no sign of her, and the chap behind the desk told him that she was not in to work that day because she was suffering from a bad cold. Fred hoped he could find other opportunities to see her in the future, but he knew that the pressures of work would keep him very busy for a long time yet.

One of the orders which had come in was for a carved mantelpiece in the drawing room of a large house near the village of Southsea between Southampton and Portsmouth. It was an unusual project, and Fred was intrigued to discover more, so having arranged a date and time for meeting his client, he set off on his bicycle one morning early in October. The house was many miles away, and before long it had started to rain. Despite the oilskin he was wearing, Fred soon felt wet and bedraggled and not at all the image he had hoped to present of himself as a well-to-do businessman. *Oh well*, he thought with some resignation, *that's life. Perhaps I should invest in a horse and carriage, and then I could arrive in a reasonable condition instead of being wet, windblown, and breathless. But then where would I keep the horse? The little plot of land at the cottage is far too small, and it would be quite expensive to hire stables.* On his long journey he also mulled over the idea of owning one of those newfangled inventions, the telephone, but of course, that would be useful only if his client owned one too. He eventually decided to concentrate on today and leave tomorrow to sort itself out.

When Fred finally arrived at the house, he was shown into a large room with a magnificent fireplace already installed. A maid took his wet coat and hat to dry them off, and his client offered him a glass of whisky to warm him up. "No, thank you, sir," Fred replied, "but if it's possible, I really would like a cup of tea." Within minutes his drink had arrived. After he had taken a few sips, Fred was shown rough drawings of his client's proposals for the mantelpiece. It was quite an intricate affair with bunches of grapes, swirls of oak leaves, and what looked like a family crest in the centre. This would test his capabilities to the limit, he thought, but he would keep that to himself and just advise that he would be more than happy to take on the commission.

"Your plan looks beautiful," he enthused. "I shall be honoured to make it for you. Let me take a few measurements, and then we must decide what kind of wood you would like. I do have some very special oak in the workshop at present, sir, but of course it's entirely up to you." Having received a nod of approval, Fred approached the question of cost. "I can only give you a rough estimate now, sir, but I will send you my definite quotation by the end of the week."

He was very taken aback when his client waved his hand and airily said, "It is of no consequence. I shall look forward to my mantelpiece being in place as soon as you are able, and I shall pay you what you ask."

I wonder what life is like when one is so rich that money is of no consequence? Fred mused on his long journey home. *Is the man happy, or is he constantly searching for something else to give him satisfaction?* He had never before met someone with such an attitude, and it intrigued him. He couldn't wait to put the question to his friends at the Carpenters Arms, but that would have to wait for another day. He just wanted to get back to Lucky and his ecstatic welcome. Earlier he had intended to go back to the workshop, but he was cold, damp, and hungry, so instead he decided to treat himself and Lucky to a fire in the small living room grate. When it had a good heat to it, he would make some toast to share. *Who needs a lot of money,* he mused, *when there is warmth and shelter and a loving companion?* A brief thought suddenly entered his startled mind that his cup of happiness would indeed be full if, in addition to Lucky, there was a loving human companion in his life. Perhaps he would examine that possibility later on. A mental image of the young librarian passed before his eyes. *Well, well!*

By evening the weather had improved, so Fred decided to walk down the lane to the Carpenters Arms to find some friendly company and enjoy a drink. Pleased to see that his friend Richard was already there, he waved to him to save him a seat whilst he went to place his order.

"It's good to see you, my friend," he exclaimed once he arrived at Richard's table. "I could do with a chat. As empathetic as Lucky might be, he doesn't have much in the way of conversation!"

Richard smiled and patted the seat next to him whilst indicating the two other men with him. "This is Nathan, and this other rogue is my cousin Henry."

"Pleased to meet you."

The four men reflectively drained their tankards in silence and then all started to talk at once. "What do you do for a living?" "Do you live near here?" "What brings you here?"

Richard laughed and explained that Fred was his friend and neighbour, then continued with a question of his own. "I saw you leaving your house very early this morning. Where were you off to at such a time?"

Fred was more than willing to share his experience, telling them about his long bicycle ride and the commission which had taken him so far, but above all, he mentioned what his client had said about the cost being of no consequence. "I warned him that it would be expensive because of the intricate carving, especially of the family crest in the centre, but he just waved his hands to dismiss it." His listeners were suitably intrigued, wondering how rich one would have to be and how they themselves would behave if they were ever in that fortunate position.

"What's his name?" asked Nathan.

"Mr Doyle," Fred replied. "I think his first name is Arthur, but I'm not sure about that."

Nathan's eyes widened. "Do you mean Arthur Conan Doyle?" he demanded.

"Yes, possibly. Why? Do you know him?"

Nathan laughed. "Don't you ever read a book, Fred? Haven't you heard of Sherlock Holmes? Mr Arthur Conan Doyle is a very celebrated author, and his Sherlock Holmes mysteries are read by thousands of people right across the world."

"I really don't have the time," Fred responded, slightly abashed, "but when I'm next in town, I'll go to the library and get one of his books, out of curiosity if nothing else." Actually his motivation in saying he would visit the library was more in the hopes of seeing the young woman again than it was any wish to read about Sherlock Holmes. But he wasn't about to admit that to his friends. He knew that any hint of a woman in his life would make him the butt of jokes and teasing comments, and at the moment he was very unsure of his emotions in that direction. However, he promised himself he would visit again very soon, and this time he would have a perfectly good excuse.

It so happened that a few weeks later, Fred had a business appointment some miles away from the workshop. He had left Lucky at home as the dog was beginning to feel his age now and was finding it more and more difficult to bound along at the pace that Fred set on his bicycle. Lucky was more than happy to snooze the day away, comfortably lying in his favourite chair. There was a water bowl nearby and food when he wanted to eat, so what more could a dog want?

Fred's meeting concluded with an order being speedily negotiated. And as it was still only eleven o'clock in the morning, instead of returning to the workshop, he decided to take the day off and visit the library. He felt a schoolboy's sense of mischief at his "truancy", and as he rode towards his destination, he started to sing some of the popular songs of the day. His repertoire was rather limited, so he sang "Sweet Rosie O'Grady" several times, followed by "After the Ball Was Over", to the amusement of the people he passed.

The country lanes gradually gave way to wider roads lined with houses, and Fred's sense of anticipation began to grow. Finally a few shops appeared, and then after a curve in the road, Fred could see the library. However, something looked different. As Fred drew up outside the building, he realised the front door was firmly shut. To his consternation, he read the notice on the door: "Closed on Mondays".

"You idiot," he said, berating himself. "Why didn't you think of that? What a waste of effort." Feeling very deflated, he turned his bicycle round in preparation to start the long journey back to Rose Cottage.

For a few moments he felt nothing but fury at his stupid lack of foresight, but then his sense of humour, never far from the surface, began to make a slow return and he started to grin. At least it would make for a good story down at the Carpenters Arms, although, of course, he would have to confess to his friends that he had little interest in Sherlock Holmes and he was actually hoping to meet a young woman at the library.

Earlier in the day, on his way into the town, Fred had noticed a small park with wide swathes of green grass and trees overhanging a lake, and he decided on impulse to buy something to eat and spend an hour or two relaxing in the sunshine. After all, he had worked very hard recently, rarely taking any time off; the paperwork was up to date; he had just secured another order; and his staff were competent enough to manage without him for a few hours. With gleeful anticipation, he bought a pastry, an apple, and a bottle of cider and then made his way back to the park. With its being a working day, the place was almost deserted and there were plenty of seats. Fred chose a wooden bench overlooking the lake and gave himself up to the peace of his surroundings. *When was I last able to relax like this?* he mused. *I really should try to do it more often. Take advantage of the works being closed on Sundays and not go into the empty office to work all day as I do most weeks.* He slowly ate his impromptu meal, brushing away the crumbs and smiling at the ducks that appeared from nowhere, quacking loudly and waddling importantly about his feet. He spread his arms along the back of the bench, lifted his face to the sun, and closed his eyes.

Twenty

It must have been nearly an hour later when Fred awoke with a start from his refreshing nap and reluctantly decided it was time to remount his bicycle and make for home. Although the park was still almost deserted, his eyes alighted on a figure in the distance. She was strolling along by the side of the lake, occasionally throwing sticks into the water for her small dog to retrieve. The dog would rush after them, barking with excitement and furiously wagging his tail, especially when told, "Good boy!" At first, as Fred later admitted to himself, he was rather annoyed at this intrusion into his peace. However, as the young woman came nearer, he slowly came to the realisation that this was the young woman from the library. What a stroke of luck! What if she didn't recognise him and just kept on walking by? *Quick, Fred, think, think!* In the next few seconds, however, his dilemma was solved when the dog came straight up to where he was sitting and planted his paws firmly on Fred's knees. "Down, Bertie, down," ordered the dog's flustered owner. Turning to Fred, she said, "I'm so sorry. I do apologise. Has my dog left dirty marks?"

"Oh no," he replied, with easy laughter bubbling up. "I also own a dog, and your dog must have picked up his scent on my clothes."

The young woman from the library then looked intently at Fred and said, "Do please excuse me if I'm being impertinent, but haven't I seen you somewhere before?"

"Yes, we have met before," replied a greatly relieved Fred. "Please, would you like to sit down? I will refresh your memory."

The young woman promptly sat on the bench next to Fred, settled her skirts about her, and then looked enquiringly at him. "I'm ready. Please go on." Fred proceeded to remind her that he had visited the library and asked for copies of the *Dorset Echo* to be shown to him. "Yes, I remember," she said. "You looked so upset and so vulnerable that day, and I wished I could do something to help you. What was it that you wanted to read in the newspaper?"

"If you can spare the time, I'd like to tell you the whole story." She nodded.

For the next half hour, Fred poured out his story. She occasionally touched his arm in sympathy but remained silent until he had at last come to a halt, saying, "And that's why I was so distressed at the library that day."

Her brown eyes full of compassion, the young woman said, "What a dreadful tragedy. And you were so young at the time. Thank you for telling me now. That was very brave of you." Looking rather puzzled, she continued, "But why are you here today? Was there something else you wanted to read? Didn't you know that the library is closed on Mondays?"

"I know that now." Fred laughed. "But if I may be so bold, the reason I came back was to try to find you again. I did come before, but you weren't at the library that day because, as I was informed, you had a bad cold."

"Oh yes. I remember my brother saying that someone had been asking for me, but I didn't know it was you!"

By this time, the day had turned decidedly chilly and the light was already beginning to fade. With great reluctance, Fred said that he really should start his journey home. "My dog, Lucky, will be wondering where I am," he explained.

"And my parents will be sending out a search party" was the laughing reply.

"I don't even know your name," said Fred, "although I told you mine at the beginning of my story. I would count it as the greatest honour if you would agree to meet me again."

She smiled. "My name is Elizabeth Marchant, but everyone calls me Lizzie. And yes, I would love to see you again."

"Will you be here next Sunday?" Fred asked hesitantly.

"Of course," Lizzie replied. "Bertie and I will be taking our usual walk about midday, and it would be really nice if you happened to be sitting there on that bench at that time." She smiled as she explained that her parents considered the little dog as good a chaperone as any human because he could be quite fearsome if he took a dislike to someone or felt his owner was uneasy about something. Consequently, she was allowed a great deal more freedom than her friends.

Fred rose to his feet and prepared to cycle away, but on impulse he lifted Lizzie's hand and daringly dropped a light kiss on it. "Until next Sunday," he said before he rode off, leaving Lizzie somewhat stunned by his bold gesture but secretly rather pleased. As she walked home, she pondered with amazement how life could change so dramatically and in such a short time, as she was very sure that Fred was going to be part of her future.

As for Fred, he smiled all the way back to Rose Cottage, and the next day at work he whistled or sang under his breath until one of his crew remarked, "You sound cheerful, Fred. Good day yesterday?"

"Yes, indeed," he replied. "I'll tell you about it some time." The fact was, however, that he was bursting to tell someone right now. As usual, Lucky had been ecstatic when Fred had arrived home, giving short barks of pleasure and wagging his tail, but he had proved disappointingly unresponsive to Fred's happy news. The week stretched ahead and the days seemed to crawl towards the following Sunday, although Fred and his staff were very busy.

The business was flourishing, and as a result of recommendations from satisfied customers, commissions and orders were flooding in. Fred became convinced that the time had come to make a decision. Either he could take on more staff or else consider in more detail the pipe dream which he shared with his friend Richard to set up in business together as house builders. They had touched on the subject quite a few times before, but Fred had never really considered it seriously. For one thing, they would need larger premises, and for another, it would be necessary to employ reliable bricklayers, stonemasons, and other experts. Richard was a valued company employee but had no private means to invest in the scheme. Could the present business of Brown & Lee sustain such an outlay on its own? Possibly not. Maybe, therefore, they would have to apply for a loan. But how would they go about that? With these questions whirling around in his mind, Fred decided to call on Richard as soon as possible to have a serious discussion about the idea.

Twenty-one

At last Sunday morning dawned. It was another bright day, but there was a definite chill in the air. Fred wondered how much longer he and Lizzie would be able to sit in the park in any comfort as winter was coming. He soon discovered that there was a stiff breeze blowing and that it was going to take him longer to reach his destination. Nearly half an hour late, he finally rode into the park, feeling a great sense of anticipation, which immediately dissipated when he could see no sign of Lizzie. Had she regretted her promise to meet him again? Had she reconsidered the whole episode and decided that she didn't want to continue their acquaintance? In despair, Fred dropped down on the bench with his back bent and his hands drooping between his knees as he wondered what to do next. He didn't know where Lizzie and her family lived. What a fool he had been not to have asked for her address, but then perhaps it was just as well if he was unwelcome.

So lost in his misery was he that he failed to notice Lizzie and her little dog standing in front of him. "Penny for your thoughts, Fred!" She laughed. "Why are you looking so miserable?"

Fred jumped to his feet, almost stumbling in his great relief. "I thought you weren't coming, that you had changed your mind. I can't tell you how relieved I am to see you. I've been counting the days."

Lizzie put her hand on his arm, saying, "I'm so sorry I worried you, but it was rather cold waiting here, so I took Bertie for a little walk." With a smile she added, "O ye of little faith, Fred. I must say, it didn't cross my mind that you might not come."

Lizzie went on to say, "Last week when I returned home, my parents asked why I had been out for such a long time, so I told them about meeting you. Although they know I am sensible, they were obviously concerned, so now they would like to meet you in person."

Fred nodded his head in agreement. "Your parents have every right to be apprehensive. And I would very much like to have the opportunity to try and set their minds at rest."

Together they made their way out of the park. A five-minute walk brought them to a rather imposing three-storey house with a flight of stone steps leading to the front door. Before Lizzie could take out her key, the door was flung open by her brother, who exclaimed, "You must be Fred. I'm Matthew, Matt for short. How do you do? We've met before very briefly, although I don't expect you remember."

"Oh, indeed I do," replied Fred, holding out his hand. "You dashed my hopes of seeing your sister when I called at the library and you said she was at home with a bad cold!"

Matt chuckled before saying, "Bring your bicycle in. You can leave it in the hall, where it won't be in the way. And then come into the parlour and meet our parents."

Fred and Lizzie were ushered into a large room where there was a fire blazing in the hearth. Mr and Mrs Marchant stood to welcome Fred and to introduce themselves. "We don't stand on ceremony in this house. We are John and Harriet, and we are pleased to meet the young man who has caused such a disturbance in our daughter's life. May we call you Fred?" They shook hands with him and then sat down again, indicating that the younger ones should do the same.

"It's the cook's day off," announced Harriet, "so we have already eaten a light lunch. Are you hungry, Fred? Because there is a large pan of soup in the kitchen all ready to heat up and serve."

Fred, who was indeed very hungry and thirsty, couldn't help saying, "That would be wonderful. I was so eager to get going this morning that I only had a slice of bread and an apple for breakfast."

Lizzie was immediately despatched to the kitchen to see to the soup, whilst her parents embarked on a series of questions directed at Fred.

"You must forgive us," said John, "but we couldn't help but feel a little concerned. It seems that Lizzie has done nothing but talk about you ever since last week. She told us about the terrible tragedy which befell your family when you were only twenty years old." He shook his head soberly before continuing. "It must have been utterly appalling for you, but to your great credit, you managed to cope. We also know that you have a dog called Lucky and that nowadays you own a carpentry business. And that is more or less the bare bones of it! So, perhaps you could tell us now what your business prospects are like and where you live. Please don't think I'm being impolite, but our daughter is very precious to us."

With great relief, Fred found himself warming to this down-to-earth couple. He began to answer their questions with all sincerity and openness. He told them how his career had flourished, owing to the generosity of his former boss, and furthermore about how he had come to own his little house thanks to the inheritance from Dora. "So, you see," he concluded, "I have also been extremely fortunate in my life. Losing my family was indeed a terrible blow, and I shall always miss them, but life goes on. In time it has become easier to bear. I am ambitious and have plans for my business, which perhaps you would allow me to discuss with you some time later." Fred then described the circumstances which had taken him to the library in the first place, and then he mentioned the excuse he had used for his second visit.

"So, you have met Arthur Conan Doyle!" exclaimed Harriet. "He must be a very ingenious man to be able to think up all those plots. Did you ever read one of his books?"

"Alas, I must confess I have not," Fred replied. "When I go home at night, I take Lucky for a walk, have a snack, take a quick bath, and then fall into bed to sleep until morning. I never seem to have much time left to read."

"We shall have to do something about that." Harriet smiled. "Has Lizzie told you that my husband owns the library?" Fred did not know this, but he quickly realised that was the reason why Lizzie and Matt both worked there. "Matt only goes in occasionally. He is struggling to become an accountant. Who knows, you might find him useful one of these days!"

Fred hoped with all his heart that he had made a good impression on Lizzie's parents. They were obviously a close-knit family, all of them eager to look out for one another, and he envied that fact very much indeed. He sensed they liked him, and they had reacted to his story with a great deal of empathy. At the moment he was thinking this, Lizzie entered the room carrying a tray upon which was a bowl of steaming soup, a large chunk of freshly made bread, and a piece of cheese almost the size of Fred's hand. "I'm sorry to have been rather a long time," she said, "but Bertie demanded to be fed first."

"Eat up, lad," said John. "You need good food inside you to face your ride back. Harriet and I are happy to invite you here next Sunday for a proper meal—if you can spare the time, that is." He had a twinkle in his eyes as he made the invitation. In the way of happily married couples, Harriet and John had already silently agreed that they liked this young man. He seemed hard-working, straight-talking, and honest, and he was obviously smitten with their daughter, whilst Lizzie in turn was quietly blossoming in his company.

Now that he knew Lizzie's address, Fred began to send her little notes by post telling her about his day and anything else which he thought would interest her. Happy to have this contact, Lizzie responded in like manner, and in this way they began to know each other well, coming to understand each other's likes and dislikes and also exchanging harmless personal jokes. Fred had let slip that by his next visit he would be a year older and was very touched to find that Lizzie and her mother had prepared a celebratory meal for him. Not only that, but also Lizzie gave him a beautiful hand-knitted scarf, whilst Harriet produced a copy of *A Study in Scarlet* by Arthur Conan Doyle. With a little chuckle, Harriet said, "I hope you will find the time to read this. It's very good." Fred felt rather overwhelmed by it all. It had been many years now since he had shared in the joys of having a loving family around him to celebrate such occasions. He still missed all his family dreadfully, but now he dared to hope that one day in the future he might indeed be the member of another loving family. His eyes rested on Lizzie and her parents.

Twenty-two

Not long after Fred's birthday, something happened which could have been catastrophic. During the winter months, he allowed a small fire to be lit in the workshop on the premise that if his staff were warm and comfortable, they would produce a better job. The fire was contained within a grate and had the protection of a wire mesh screen around it, so it was deemed entirely safe. On this day, however, one of the apprentices had removed the screen to add another log and had neglected to replace the screen. As the log settled, a few sparks flew out, landing on a pile of sawdust a little distance away. A blaze erupted immediately, and were it not for the speedy action of the men working nearby, the workshop could have suffered serious damage. Although the premises were covered by insurance, Fred acknowledged that had the fire taken hold, the business itself might not have survived.

His indecision about joining up in business with Richard vanished immediately. Of course it was the right thing to do. How could he have doubted it for one minute? A second workplace would safeguard all their jobs, and he strongly believed that the venture would prove successful. That evening when he returned home, he could barely wait to knock on Richard's door to impart the news of his decision. He was confident that Richard would agree to his plans because he had always shown great enthusiasm for the idea.

"Hello, my friend!" exclaimed Richard as he opened the door. "What brings you here at this time of night? Come and sit down."

Fred made himself comfortable and then proceeded to tell Richard about the events of that day and, consequently, of the momentous decision he had made. "But only if you are still interested," Fred said anxiously.

"Of course I am," Richard answered immediately. "You must have known how eager I've always been, but I felt I should leave it to you to make the final decision because, after all, it will be your company funding it to a great extent. It will be a challenge, and it will probably cost far more than we can afford, but it's a great opportunity. We simply must not let it slip through our fingers."

The two men sat and talked far into the night, excitedly discussing their plans, albeit with a slightly nervous edge, until Fred finally stood up to stretch his legs, saying, "I must get to bed now, and so must you. We have to be up again in three hours' time."

Over the following three or four months, both men worked tirelessly, not only on their project, but also with their ongoing jobs. They jokingly agreed that a good night's sleep was becoming a luxury they could ill afford, but somehow they kept going. They experienced many changes of mood, from great optimism to appalled shock at what they had taken on. Fred insisted on keeping his Sundays free to visit Lizzie whenever possible, but in January and February that year there were several heavy snowfalls which prevented his taking the bicycle out, and they had to make do with writing daily letters to one another. Fortunately, the postal system was very good, and whatever the weather, their notes were delivered the next day, sometimes even by the afternoon of the same day. Fred longed to end his letters, "With all my love", but had not yet found the courage. He did, however, dare to address them to "My Dearest Lizzie".

Before that, Harriet and John had invited Fred to join them for Christmas, but with great reluctance he had declined, explaining that he always visited his only relatives, his aunt Ann and uncle William and their family, and they would be disappointed if he didn't join them this time. In truth, Fred felt rather guilty that he had not called upon them for many months now. He had written a note, however, telling them all about his business project, but he didn't mention that he had a young woman in his life. If Aunt Ann knew about his feelings for Lizzie, she wouldn't have given him any peace until she had wormed every last detail out of him!

Christmas Day that year had fallen on a Friday, so Fred had given his staff a generous four-day break from work. Most of the men were very grateful and looked forward to spending some leisure time, but one or two of them grumbled. "What on earth am I going to do with myself all that time? The wife will moan about me being under her feet, and the children will get on my nerves." Once Christmas Day was over, Fred planned to stay with Lucky in the peace and warmth of his little cottage and tackle the mountain of paperwork that never seemed to get any smaller.

Twenty-three

Finally, on a hot summer's day in June 1886, their dreams and plans came to fruition when Fred and Richard stood in front of their heavily mortgaged premises and watched a brand new sign being erected:

HANCOCK & LEE
High-Quality
Builders and Carpenters

The two of them had previously discussed whose name should appear first and agreed that "Hancock & Lee" rolled off the tongue more easily. For the following two weeks they arrived early in the morning at their new offices in a great state of excitement and anticipation, but to their dismay business was extremely slow to come in. Indeed, there had been only two requests for quotations and one definite order which had come from one of Fred's previous customers. Their euphoria soon disappeared and they began to worry about the possibility of their having made a colossal mistake. Despite all their efforts, it was very difficult to remain optimistic.

Then one day towards the end of July, a gleaming horseless carriage drew up outside and an expensive-looking gentleman emerged. Fred and Richard stared open-mouthed at the automobile as they had never before seen one of these amazing machines at such close quarters. Quickly regaining their composure, they greeted their visitor.

"Good morning, sir. Please come in and take a seat. How can we help you?"

"My name is Robert Dunbar," the man replied. "I am a factory owner. I have purchased a large area of land near the factory on which I propose to build a village for my workers. Initially it will consist of about fifty houses, a small school, and one or two stores." Fred listened to this explanation with astonishment and growing excitement, although he felt he first had to ask Mr Dunbar why he had chosen their company to quote for such a lucrative job. After all, there were many other construction firms which had been established for a far longer time. Mr Dunbar laughed and replied, "I like your honesty, Mr Lee. In truth, I am a somewhat unconventional person, and I chose you because of your names. My wife's name was Hancock before she married me, and I do wonder if there might be some connection back in the past. As for you, Mr Lee, I remember reading some years ago about a shipping tragedy where six of the victims had the same name. Would that have been anything to do with you, by any chance?"

"Yes, sir." Fred nodded. "My parents and four sisters all drowned when the *Avalanche* sank."

"My apologies if I have upset you."

Fred waved his hand in acknowledgement. "It was a long time ago now, and although I will never forget them, I have learned to live without them. Now, sir, would you care to discuss your plans in more detail?"

"An architect has already made some drawings for me." Mr Dunbar went on after a pause, saying, "I will leave them with you, but please take great care as they are the only copies I have at present." He continued to outline his vision of Dunbar Village, as it was to be called, but after about an hour he suddenly stood up and announced that he would have to be on his way now. "I look forward to receiving your quotation and to doing business with you both." Then he strode off towards his automobile, which in the meantime, of course, had attracted a large number of curious onlookers. With a great clatter and a scattering of his audience, Mr Dunbar drove off.

Fred and Richard looked at one another and burst out laughing. "Well, I never! What an extraordinary gentleman!" Richard exclaimed. "But you know, Fred, I do believe he is a genuine philanthropist. It would give a huge boost to our reputation if he decides to go ahead."

"But are we capable of such a big project, Richard? If it goes wrong, we're finished. But on the other hand, if it goes right ..." He trailed off and suddenly grinned. "I'm going to leave the decision to you, Richard." Fred knew before he had finished speaking that he very much wanted to take up the challenge, but he realised that Richard would have to be equally enthusiastic.

Richard nodded his head. "We'll have to consider this very carefully. Take our time to discuss all the pros and all the cons. We mustn't rush into it." A few minutes later he turned to Fred with a beaming smile stretching from ear to ear and said, "I've considered. Let's do it."

Fred eagerly looked forward to telling Lizzie all about their somewhat eccentric visitor and the proposition he had put forward.

Twenty-four

The following Sunday was a warm and pleasant day in early August. Fred and Lizzie set off for a stroll around the park, finally sitting down on their customary bench. For several moments they sat in companionable silence until Lizzie could bear it no longer. "Out with it!" she said. "I can tell you have something to tell me. You've hardly responded to a word I've said, and you seem very distracted."

Glad to have the opportunity to impart his important news, Fred began to tell her all about the events of the previous week, making her smile at his description of Mr Dunbar.

"That's wonderful news, my dear. You and Richard must be so proud of yourselves." Her eyes shone with happiness for him.

On impulse, he turned to her and blurted out, "Lizzie Marchant. How does the idea of changing your name to Lizzie Lee appeal to you?"

Lizzie looked at him wide-eyed and smiled before saying, "Fred Lee. If that was a proposal of marriage, then you will have to do a lot better than that."

Thus emboldened, Fred took her hand and knelt down on the rough gravel, to the amusement of several passers-by. "Elizabeth Marchant," he said as seriously as he could manage with such a big smile on his face, "I love you with all my heart. Will you do me the honour of becoming my wife?"

From their unexpected audience came several piercing whistles and shouts of, "Go on, say yes!" And they clapped their approval when they heard her joyful reply.

"Oh, my darling, of course I will."

Fred rose to his feet and gently kissed the lips of his new fiancée. "I should have asked for your father's permission first," he said, worried, "but you looked so adorable, I couldn't help myself."

"My parents will be delighted," Lizzie reassured him. "As you know, they don't stand on ceremony, and for weeks now they've been hinting about any news. Come on, let's go and tell them."

As they arrived back at the house, they saw that Harriet and John were in the front garden enjoying the sunshine. One look at the happy faces in front of them told them all they hoped to hear. Harriet kissed Fred soundly on both cheeks, whilst John shook his hand warmly. "Congratulations, my boy," he said. "Welcome to our family. We couldn't be happier."

The following year passed in a blur of frenzied activity for Fred. He and Richard had received the plans and preliminary drawings for Dunbar Village, and their first concern was to employ good, reliable workers. The financial outlay was tremendous, but somehow their books balanced at the end of every month, thanks mainly to the carpentry business. Fred had realised quite early on that he would not be able to manage the company of Brown & Lee and also deal with this huge new undertaking, so he approached his old boss Samuel Brown to ask if Samuel could possibly help out, just on a temporary basis. He was nervous about such temerity but soon discovered that Samuel was delighted to accept. After some eighteen months of retirement, Samuel said he had to admit that he was becoming extremely bored. For a while he had thoroughly enjoyed visiting London and the countryside and having the freedom to go out and about, but the feeling had begun to pale, and he missed the daily challenges and the camaraderie of the workshop. He often found himself at a loose end at home because his wife had many female friends whom she visited on a regular basis. He occasionally sat down and tried to read a book, but his mind would wander and the story never held his attention. The long and short of it was that he had found retirement rather irksome, and to return to the workshop was a dream come true.

In the meantime, Lizzie was quietly making arrangements for the wedding, which was to take place at her local church towards the end of September. Neither she nor Fred wanted an elaborate affair, so the guest list was limited to very close relatives and some cherished friends, in all about thirty people. Fearing that Fred's workload would prevent their having a honeymoon, Lizzie was delighted when he suggested a week away "wherever you please", promising that he would not go back to work or even think about his business until they returned home.

Lizzie naively responded, "And I too will take time off from the library."

She was rather taken aback when Fred firmly replied, "But surely you'll give up your job when we are married? I don't want my wife working when I can well afford to keep her in some style."

"Fred," replied Lizzie equally firmly, "I'm sorry you don't like the idea of my working, but I intend to do so, for the time being at least."

Fred looked at her for the moment and then broke into a grin. "I do believe we've had our first disagreement. Let's leave it for now, shall we?"

The question of where they would live was troubling Fred. Rose Cottage had been adequate for a bachelor, but it was far too small for a couple—and hopefully a family one day. He could afford to rent a much bigger house or, dare he even think it, follow the new trend of buying his own home. The trouble was that he just didn't have time at the moment to explore the possibilities.

One day he voiced his concerns to his future in-laws, and once again he noticed a secret look passing between them.

"We have been thinking about that, Fred," said Harriet, "and if the idea is acceptable to you and Lizzie, we would be very happy to offer you the top floor of this house. It's warm up there, and there are a few bits and pieces of furniture, but it would need your personal touch to make it comfortable for you both. It's only a suggestion, and we won't be offended if you turn it down, but we thought it might ease the pressure of trying to find somewhere to live before the wedding."

"That's so kind of you!" exclaimed Fred. "It could be the perfect solution. Do you agree, Lizzie?"

Lizzie slowly nodded her head. "For the short term, yes." She turned to Harriet and John, who were waiting for her response. "Thank you both so much. It's very kind of you, and we appreciate the offer. We'll make every effort to find our own home and leave you in peace, but for the moment it is, as Fred says, the perfect solution."

Lucky was another of Fred's concerns. He was showing his age, which Fred reckoned to be about twelve years, and most likely would be unhappy about moving from his familiar surroundings to live in the top floor of a strange house. Once again, however, fate took a hand. Usually, when Fred arrived home from work in the evening, Lucky would bark a welcome and move, stiffly nowadays, across the room to meet him with his tail wagging. On this particular occasion, however, Fred opened his front door to silence and a strange stillness in the air. He knew immediately what had happened. His adorable and adoring companion of so many years was lying motionless on the floor. Fred could see that he was not breathing. He felt a terrible emptiness at the sight, wanting to sob, but the tears refused to fall. He knelt on the floor and cradled Lucky's head in his hands for a long time until a knock on the front door brought him to his feet. It was Richard.

"Hello, Fred. Is everything all right? Usually we hear Lucky bark when you come home, but tonight there was nothing, and we wondered if anything had happened."

Fred nodded and silently ushered his friend into the room. "Lucky's gone." He choked on the words. "And I wasn't here at the end. I pray that he didn't suffer and just slipped away in his sleep."

"I'm sure that was the way of it," Richard said, trying to console his friend. "Lucky looks so peaceful. Almost like a young pup again." He put his arm round Fred's shoulders and said rather hesitantly, "Shall we go into the garden now and bury him? Then I suggest we go down to the Carpenters Arms to tell our friends what has happened. You don't want to be alone now. The company may help."

Fred went through the next few days in a haze of sadness. He spent much time reminiscing about Lucky's life and the impact the dog had made on his own life. Things would have been so different if Fred had not been adopted the dog. In fact, he might not even be alive if he had agreed to emigrate to New Zealand with his family.

He sent a short note to Lizzie, and by return of post came an endearing reply, sending her sympathies and her deepest love. This had the desired effect of cheering Fred's mood. He couldn't wait to see her again.

Twenty-five

The wedding day finally arrived with the sun shining down upon the mellow autumnal landscape. Fred had tossed and turned in his bed the night before and had heard the sound of rain pouring down. *Oh no,* he had thought, groaning, *please don't let the weather spoil our day!* His relief was great when he saw how the skies had cleared. He had booked to stay in a local hotel not far from the church, so he had plenty of time to eat his breakfast and get dressed in his wedding finery. The trouble was that he felt so nervous he could only manage a slice of toast and a cup of coffee.

In the Marchant household, the atmosphere was very different. The family had previously decided to hold the reception in their large back garden, praying that the sun would shine, and Harriet had been bustling around since dawn. The proud owner of a copy of *Mrs Beeton's Book of Household Management*, she had spent many weeks now poring over the recipes, choosing ones which she hoped her guests would enjoy.

Displayed on large serving dishes were three cold poached salmon, decorated with slices of lemon and watercress and accompanied by a colourful salad. There were plates of ham and pork and plates of cheese with delicate savoury biscuits. For anybody who might have preferred a hot meal, Harriet had prepared a huge saucepan of vegetable soup with chunks of bread for dunking. Afterwards, there were fluffy meringues, raspberry tarts, and platters of seasonal fruit. John had declared himself in charge of the champagne and had ordered half a dozen bottles.

Lizzie, who seemed calm amidst all the hubbub, offered to help her mother but was firmly told, "Go away and make yourself look beautiful." She retired to the sitting room with Bertie, where she brushed his coat and tied a big red ribbon around his neck.

"Be a good boy," she whispered, "and don't try to bite it off."

Lizzie had chosen a simple white wedding dress in silk and lace, and in her hair she wore flowers from the garden. As she glided down the aisle on her father's arm, Fred reflected that he had never seen anyone look so beautiful. He loved her very much and vowed he would do everything possible to make her happy. Richard, his best man, tapped him on the shoulder to remind him to step forward, and the service began.

As the organ played Mendelssohn's Wedding March, the newly married couple stepped out into the churchyard, where a photographer had set up his equipment. "I hope this won't take long," Fred whispered optimistically. Contrary to the convention of the day, he took Lizzie in his arms. "I love you, Mrs Lee. Smile at the camera now." With the photographs duly taken, the couple mingled with their guests before running through a shower of confetti to the carriage which would take them back to Lizzie's home for the reception. Harriet and John had left a few minutes before and were waiting at the front door to welcome them, together with Bertie minus his wedding bow.

Lizzie laughed as she saw a soggy red mess on the floor. "I thought he would chew that off at the first opportunity."

Some women from the village had been employed to serve the food and drink, and the afternoon progressed with much cheer. Speeches by the father of the bride and the best man were heartily applauded, but it was Fred's loving compliments to his new wife that brought tears to the eyes of many of their guests.

Soon afterwards, Lizzie quietly left the festive group in the garden to change into her going-away outfit. Again, this was very simple, being a close-fitting cotton dress in pale pink with dozens of pearl buttons from the neck to the hem and halfway up the sleeves. To complete the outfit, her bonnet was in a matching shade of pink and had long ribbons to keep it in place. As she returned to her guests, she was greeted by claps and cheers and a beaming Fred. "You look beautiful," he said with a slight catch in his voice. "It's time to say goodbye now, Mrs Lee, because your carriage awaits." Indeed the same driver with his horse and carriage had returned to take them to the station where they would board a train to London. This had been Lizzie's somewhat surprising choice of destination for their honeymoon, and Fred had agreed without question.

Lizzie, who had never travelled by train before, wondered how she would enjoy the experience. In fact, she was fascinated by the size of the engine and the noise it made as the train came puffing along the platform edge and stopped with a squeal of its brakes. "You're like a little girl," teased Fred. "Your eyes are nearly popping out of your head." In fact, he could count on one hand the number of times he had travelled by train, and he was almost as awestruck as Lizzie.

The eighty-mile journey to London passed incredibly quickly. As the environs of the capital city began to flash by, Fred hugged his new wife to his side and exclaimed, "What an experience! Fancy coming all that way in such a short time." Within minutes the great engine puffed importantly into Waterloo Station, and Fred rose to his feet to collect their suitcases from the overhead rack.

"We'll have to find some transport to take us to our hotel," he said. "I'm not sure how far it is." Although it was evening by now, the noise of the traffic assaulted their ears as they left the station.

They surveyed the scene in some bemusement, wondering how they could possibly manage to attract the attention of any likely transport, so it was to their great relief when they heard a cheerful voice behind them calling out, "You need to go somewhere, mister? 'Op in and tell me where you're staying." Fred and Lizzie gratefully hopped in and sat back to enjoy their first experience of this busy metropolis.

Fred had been advised on good authority that Victoria was the best central point from which to explore the city, and therefore he had booked a small hotel just off the Buckingham Palace Road. As he and Lizzie arrived outside, they could see a flight of stone steps leading to an open door, beyond which was a brightly lit reception area. A smiling young woman greeted them, saying, "Welcome to the Queens Hotel. If you would be kind enough to sign in, we will show you to your room." With a flourish and an inward surge of happiness, Fred wrote "Mr and Mrs F. Lee" in the proffered register before turning to Lizzie and giving her a wink and a beaming smile. "Harry!" called the receptionist, and a small boy, who could not have been more than ten years old, appeared to escort them to their room. They learned later that he was the son of the proprietor and that he made quite a substantial contribution to the family finances with the tips he received.

Despite a mild protest from Fred, the boy picked up their suitcases and staggered off along the corridor and up a flight of stairs, finally stopping at a door a few feet along. "Here's your key," he solemnly announced. "Please leave it at the reception desk when you leave the hotel. If there is anything you need, please don't hesitate to let us know." He promptly turned and marched away, leaving Fred and Lizzie in a state of giggles.

"What a sweetie! I wonder what he will be when he grows up."

The first thing they noticed when entering their room was a sign which read, "This room is equipped with Edison electric light. Do not attempt to light with a match. Simply turn key on the wall by this door. The use of electricity is in no way harmful to health, nor does it affect the soundness of sleep."

"Wonders of the modern world," Fred marvelled. "Do you think houses in the future will be equipped with electric light? If so, Richard and I will have to find out more about it."

"Yes," agreed Lizzie, "I must say, it would be wonderful if you could just turn a key instead of all the business of lighting the gasket."

They moved further into the room and somewhat shyly regarded each other and the big double bed with its turned-down covers and plump pillows. Fred took a tentative step towards his new wife, and she towards him, until they were locked in a passionate embrace. Although Fred was inexperienced, he proved to be a considerate lover, and Lizzie happily responded to his gentle touch. As she drifted off to sleep, she thought of how very fortunate she was to have found such a wonderful man who clearly loved her as deeply as she loved him.

They awoke in the early morning to the cacophony of London traffic, which was steadily building up. "Good morning, Mrs Lee," said a smiling Fred. Propping himself up on his elbow, he continued, saying, "Our adventure begins! Where would you like to start?"

Secretly, Lizzie thought she would rather like to stay all day exactly where she was, in bed with this handsome, kindly man who was now her husband, but after a moment's consideration, she replied, "I think we should start with Buckingham Palace. We might even spot the Queen!"

After a hearty breakfast, they made their way to the front door, duly leaving their room key at the reception desk as instructed by young Harry. And at that moment, to their amusement, he appeared from the back and asked if they needed transport. Upon receiving confirmation that indeed they wished to hire a horse and carriage, Harry ran down the steps, put his fingers up to his lips, and gave a piercing whistle, which immediately attracted a passing cabby. "There you are, Mr and Mrs Lee," he said importantly. "Enjoy your day." He hovered a moment before Fred realised he was waiting for the inevitable tip.

"That young man will definitely prosper," Fred whispered to Lizzie, who was on the brink of another bout of giggles. They turned their attention to the cabby and were surprised to see that it was the same chap who had brought them to the hotel the previous evening.

"'Ello again," he said. "Fancy seeing you! Where can I take you?"

"Buckingham Palace, please."

The cabby grinned. "Off to see the old queen, are you? Well, 'op in then. It's not far. You could've walked it really, but I'm 'ere now, so we'll be on our way." After a few minutes, he continued. "Seriously, if you two are 'ere to explore London, I'd be 'appy to offer me services. I know the city like the back of me 'and."

"That's a very good idea," replied Fred, turning to Lizzie for a nod of approval before agreeing to the charge and striking a deal.

Fred and Lizzie sat on the edges of their seats for the short journey to Buckingham Palace, eager not to miss a single monument or park or well-known building. They constantly remarked on the sights they were passing. It seemed no time until their driver announced, "'Ere we are, Buck 'ouse. But I'm sorry to say it looks as if the Queen ain't at 'ome."

"'Ow, I mean *how*, do you know that?" asked Lizzie.

"'Cos there's a flag called the Royal Standard which flies over the palace when the monarch is in residence, and today it ain't there," the cabby explained. "'Er Majesty will be at Osborne 'ouse on the Isle of Wight." He'd said this as if he had inside knowledge.

Fred and Lizzie decided to take a walk up to the front gates, and for ten minutes or so they watched the sentries on duty with great interest. When they returned to their carriage, their driver was ready with the next question: "Where to now?"

"Well, you know London," replied Fred, "so why don't you take us to the places you think will interest us?" Accordingly, they were bowled down the Mall and through St James's Park to their next destination, Trafalgar Square.

Once again, the young couple were amazed at the sight of so many people congregating in one place. And they were overawed by the splendid Nelson's Column soaring 170 feet into the sky.

"Are you enjoying your day?" enquired Fred fondly, putting his arm around Lizzie's waist.

"Oh yes! It's so exciting to see the places I've only read about before. But do you know, my love, I wouldn't want to live here. I suppose London residents are used to all the commotion, but I prefer beyond doubt our little town in Hampshire." She went on: "Look at all those pigeons! There must be hundreds of them. And over there I can see a man selling packets of seed to feed them. Shall we?"

They finally returned to their patient horse and driver, only to find that the driver had fallen asleep. They exchanged amused glances. "Shall we wake him?" But at that moment, he gave a great snort and sat up looking rather embarrassed.

"Sorry about that, sir," he said. "I don't know wot came over me. Anyway, where to now?"

Before answering the question, Fred asked, "Would you mind telling us your name? You know that we are Mr and Mrs Lee, but informally we are Fred and Lizzie."

"And I'm Jack Newton. And my 'orse is Molly." They all shook hands. With the pleasantries concluded, Fred and Lizzie decided to make one more visit before returning to their hotel.

"I'm rather hungry, actually," Fred admitted. "Perhaps you could take us to a restaurant for something to eat."

"Simpson's ain't far away," replied Jack, "and I 'ear they serve very good food. Mind you, I've never been in there meself. Or else there's Rules Restaurant near Covent Garden. That's not far away either."

Their light meal turned out to be far more expensive than they had expected, which concerned Lizzie. "We can't do this every day," she protested. "It's an awful waste of money. Perhaps tomorrow we can find a shop to buy some sandwiches. And I'm sure the hotel will provide an evening meal if we ask, or"—she giggled—"we could mention it to Harry."

As Jack and Molly brought the Lees back to the hotel, the couple discussed their plans for the next day. "Do you know," said Lizzie, "I rather fancy visiting the zoological gardens in Regents Park. Is that all right, Jack?"

"Of course, I'll be back tomorrow at 'alf past ten." And with a wave of his whip, he bade them farewell.

When the couple emerged from the hotel the next morning, Jack was already waiting for them. As they trotted off, he commented, "You're lucky the sun is shining. You wouldn't want to be walking around in the rain. As it is, may I suggest that as you'll need several hours to see it all, I'll return for you at four o'clock. Would that suit you?"

"Yes, of course, we'll be waiting here at the gates," was the reply.

From the moment they entered the gardens, Lizzie was amazed at the sight of all the extraordinary animals she had only read about in books. "Look! There's an elephant! And lions and tigers! And giraffes!

And just watch those monkeys leaping about!" Fred was similarly impressed but was rather less excitable, although he found Lizzie's exuberance very endearing. He took her hand and lightly kissed it, then was rewarded by a glowing look from his wife.

It was a warm day. After a couple of hours, they decided to take a brief rest if they could find an unoccupied seat. Luck was with them as ten minutes later they were relaxing under the shade of an enormous tree.

A few yards away a stallholder was shouting out, "Come now, ladies and gents. Try my pie and mash. It's the best in town."

"Shall we?" enquired Fred, their previous plan to buy sandwiches having come to nothing. At a nod from Lizzie, he strolled over and purchased two helpings of the famous London East End pie and mash. They agreed it was delicious.

Lizzie remarked, "Just wait until I tell my friends that I've eaten a traditional London pie and mash. They will be so envious!" She went on to warn Fred, "But don't expect me to try jellied eels. I will have to draw the line there."

Having sat for some time enjoying the sights, sounds, and smells of the zoological gardens, Fred consulted his pocket watch and said, "I think we've got time to see one more animal, and then we shall have to leave. So, what will it be?"

"Something exotic," Lizzie replied. She almost collapsed with laughter when they rounded a corner to discover a herd of hippos wallowing in the muddy shores of a small lake. "Ah well." She chuckled. "Perhaps they appear exotic in their own world." As the couple walked through the gates, they saw that Jack was already waiting for them.

"'Ave a good day?" he enquired.

"Wonderful! We have had the most amazing day, and we've enjoyed every moment of it. We shall have so many memories when we return home." Fred squeezed Lizzie's hand in agreement.

It was pouring with rain when the Lees awoke on the third day of their honeymoon, so after a leisurely breakfast, they decided to visit the British Museum. Unfortunately, within a very short time, they agreed with one another that it was all rather dry and, to tell the truth, boring.

"Perhaps Jack could take us to that big store in Knightsbridge that I've heard so much about," Lizzie suggested. "It's called Harrods, and their boast is that they can fill any order one cares to give them."

"Perhaps we should order an elephant," Fred suggested with a smile.

"Oh, silly you! What would we do with an elephant at home?" Lizzie laughingly replied.

Harrods proved to be a veritable fairyland for Lizzie, who moved from floor to floor exclaiming about the immense range of goods on sale. She longingly handled a beautiful silk dress but decided she couldn't possibly justify the cost. However, when they finally left Harrods and had climbed into their waiting carriage, Fred pretended that he had left something behind.

"Wait here with Jack. I won't be a minute," he said to Lizzie.

That evening the dress was delivered to their hotel, and Lizzie was overwhelmed with love for her husband. "You are the kindest, dearest man," she exclaimed, "and I love you very, very much."

Before that, however, they still had an afternoon free. The rain had cleared away, leaving the roads and buildings looking clean and fresh. "'Perhaps 'yde Park," suggested Jack. "It'll look good now the rain 'as stopped." Indeed, the trees and grass were a vibrant green, and the Serpentine sparkled in the rays of the sun. The flowerbeds were a mass of colour. As Lizzie admired them, she thought that Londoners were very fortunate to have so many green spaces around them to counteract the noise of the city itself. She was completely unaware, of course, of the underside of London, including the poverty and despair of many of its inhabitants.

The couple strolled along the paths and the lake, stopping frequently to admire the view and to watch the ducks and swans being fed by groups of excited youngsters. At one point they came across an ice-cream seller. Lizzie was amused to see the children flocking round the cart, eager to buy a penny lick.

"Listen!" she said at one point. "I think I can hear music." And indeed, ahead of them there was a barrel organ belting out tunes from the past and present. An appreciative crowd had gathered, many of whom were humming and tapping their feet along with the music.

After ten minutes, the hurdy-gurdy man announced, "That's all, folks," and began to pass his hat around for tips. Fred dropped a coin in, and there were contributions from a few others, but some of the audience began to melt away. The man shrugged with disappointment.

"Oh, how mean!" exclaimed Lizzie. "Fred, why don't you put in another penny?"

"You have such a soft heart," he said teasingly as he complied.

Late in the afternoon, Fred and Lizzie reached Rotten Row, where they stood for a while watching the aristocrats and important people ride their horses up and down. "I wonder why it's called Rotten Row?" Lizzie wondered, but for once Fred didn't have an answer.

As they arrived back at their hotel, Lizzie turned to Fred and said rather impulsively, "I've been thinking, my dear. We've had a wonderful few days here in London, and we've seen some amazing sights, but quite honestly, I find the constant noise and bustle rather unsettling. Would you very much mind if we returned home a day or so early?"

"That's exactly what I've been thinking," Fred replied, "but I've another idea to put to you." He went on to tell Lizzie of his long-held desire to visit the little church in Southwell which had been built in memory of all those who had drowned in the *Avalanche* disaster. "We could take the train down to Weymouth, book a hotel for a couple of days, and then find some transport to get us to Southwell."

Secretly, Lizzie would have preferred to go straight home, but she agreed without question, knowing how much the experience would mean to her beloved husband.

Twenty-six

The first thing that Fred noticed when they arrived at the church was the rusting anchor propped up outside. Being the only part of the ship that had been salvaged from the wreck, it had acquired a huge significance. He learned that the church had been erected on this exact spot because it overlooked the area where the *Avalanche* had floundered. As he and Lizzie moved inside the church, their eyes fell immediately on three beautiful stained glass windows depicting various aspects of the tragedy, including one of the fourteen brave fishermen who rowed out from Chesil Cove in such treacherous weather in an effort to find any survivors. Indeed, they managed to rescue twelve men from the *Forest* and brought them safely back to shore. On the wall of the church there was an artist's impression of those survivors stumbling up the beach. Of course, Fred had already heard all about these incredible acts of courage and was very glad to know that the fishermen had been handsomely rewarded. There were many other memorials, including a brass tablet engraved with the names of all those who had perished. Fred kissed his fingers and ran them lightly over the names of his family. With tears gathering in his eyes, he turned to Lizzie and admitted, "It is all becoming rather too poignant. I've seen everything I want to see, so please, shall we go now?"

They arrived home the following day, to be greeted by a smiling Harriet and John and an ecstatic Bertie.

Twenty-seven

It seemed to Fred that the past week had been just a dream. Now that they were back from their honeymoon, life continued as before, with one exception, of course, which was that he now had the great joy of snuggling up to Lizzie in bed at night and making sweet love to her. Even then, sometimes he was too weary after an exceptionally busy day at the works to do anything but eat his supper and then fall fast asleep.

Dunbar Village was beginning to take shape with the foundations of the first six houses having already been laid. For all his apparent eccentricity, Mr Dunbar proved to be a very astute businessman, so much so that Fred and Richard formed a great respect for him and listened intently to all his plans. It was he who had suggested building just six houses initially, followed by another six and so on until the project was complete. "It will be good for my workers' morale," he explained, "to see the completed homes and to understand that this was no empty promise on my part to provide for them. Furthermore, I intend to allot the houses on an informal and entirely random basis so there is no ill feeling or murmurs of favouritism."

Local businessmen were beginning to notice the development of Dunbar Village. They agreed that this new building company of Hancock & Lee looked promising, and soon they were queueing up to ask for quotations on various projects of their own. Fred and Richard took on more staff, including three clerical workers to take over most of the paperwork, They also explored the possibility of employing one of the new breed of professionals—an electrician. There were plans for the outskirts of Southampton to be developed quite rapidly, and they hoped that a great deal of the business would come their way.

Whilst Fred was away from home for twelve hours a day, Lizzie had quietly returned to her job at the library. Fred had finally given in to her argument that as it was owned by her father, she had every right to help out. In fact, she was very glad to have something to occupy her as she had discovered that life in the top-floor flat was somewhat tedious and she found it very difficult to fill her days, Harriet was downstairs, of course, but she was busy with her own household affairs, and Lizzie felt she shouldn't intrude.

Lizzie had been back at the library for about a month when one afternoon a middle-aged woman came in and asked to speak to her. "Does this library take second-hand books?" she asked. "You see, my dear mother passed away recently, and she has left a great quantity of books. They are all in very good condition, but I just don't know what to do with them. I don't want any money for them. It just seems such a dreadful shame to throw them away when somebody else might appreciate them."

Lizzie replied that she would be happy to take any books that were suitable and suggested that she call round to assess them. Almost as an afterthought, she asked if the woman would be moving into her mother's home.

"Oh no," the woman replied, "my husband and I live in a very nice house on the other side of town. Once we have emptied her house of the furniture and got rid of all those books, we shall try to sell it."

Lizzie paused for no more than a second before saying, "I do hope you don't think I'm being rude, but could I possibly come and look at the house before you put it on the market? You see, my husband and I have only been married a few weeks, and we're virtually living in my parents' home until we can find somewhere of our own. Could you tell me a little about your mother's house and possibly how much money you will ask for it?"

"It's at the end of a short terrace, and it has a small garden front and back," the woman replied. "Downstairs there are two reception rooms and a kitchen/scullery, whilst upstairs there are three bedrooms and a large bathroom, which has a flushing lavatory. My mother was very proud of that! I can't give you a price, because my husband and I haven't discussed it yet, but at a rough guess I would say about a hundred pounds. Do you think you and your husband might be interested?"

"I will ask him this evening," promised Lizzie. "It sounds ideal for us, but obviously the decision will be his to make."

That evening Lizzie waited impatiently for Fred to arrive home. He had barely stepped into the room when she said, "Fred, I think I may have found a house for us! I'm longing to tell you all about it, but I'll wait until you sit down for your supper and we can talk properly."

Fred, understanding how excited she was, promptly sat down. "Right, Mrs Lee, I'm all ears. Tell me now."

Lizzie proceeded to explain the events of her day, concluding with, "I've arranged to go and look at the books next Monday, so I'll be able to see the house at the same time. What do you think?"

Fred slowly nodded his head, eager not to burst Lizzie's bubble of enthusiasm. "It sounds just right for us, but go steady. The reality might be too awful to contemplate. Still, there's no harm in looking it over, and it does sound promising. How much did you say they will be asking?"

"About a hundred pounds."

"We could possibly manage that, but it will be scraping the bottom of the barrel."

Lizzie smiled and gave her husband a hug. "Thank you for even thinking about it. I can't wait until next Monday."

Within eight weeks, the little house was officially theirs, but it still needed a thorough clean. They had asked the old woman's daughter if they could buy the furniture, but she said she didn't want anything for it and it would be doing her a favour if they were to take it off her hands. Not all the furniture was to their taste, of course, being heavy and dark, but they agreed it would do very well for the time being. The exception was a splendid dining room table and six chairs fashioned in walnut which the carpenters at Hancock

& Lee had secretly made as a wedding present for the couple. Fred had been astounded when they had presented it to him back in the summer, and it also humbled him quite a bit that they should apparently have thought so highly of him. The dining room set had been stored at the workshop ever since, but now it took pride of place in the front room.

Christmas was only two weeks away, so Fred and Lizzie decided not to move in until the New Year, when everything was quiet again. "We can spend Christmas Day here with my family and Boxing Day over at the house putting everything in order. That is, if you agree, Fred," Lizzie suggested somewhat anxiously as she recognised that any spare time was very precious to him. "I've got lots of things in my bottom drawer to take to the house. I've been collecting them ever since I first dreamed of my wedding, things like towels, linens, some pots and pans, and lots of ornaments. Isn't this all so exciting! Just fancy, a house of our own!"

The weather that Christmas was remarkably mild, and the move to their new house took place on 2nd January without any hitches. Fred insisted on carrying Lizzie over the threshold. As he swung her up in his arms, he declared, "You are as light as a feather, my dearest girl."

Lizzie laughed. "You won't think so in a few months' time." She had been waiting for the right moment to tell Fred of her suspicion that she might be expecting a baby, and this seemed to be the perfect opportunity.

"What do you mean?" asked Fred with puzzlement written all over his face, before the penny slowly dropped. He lit up with joy as he gently lowered his wife to the ground and soundly kissed her. "You must go and sit down," he said. "I'll see to everything from now on."

"Don't be silly, Fred. I'm not ill. In fact, I feel very well, and I really don't want to be mollycoddled. Maybe I'll need a little help when the baby is born, but we'll cross that bridge when we come to it."

The next day they returned to the Marchant family home to

collect some more bits and pieces, but more importantly to tell Harriet and John their exciting news.

"That's simply wonderful!" enthused Harriet. "John! What do you think of that? We're going to be grandparents!"

John smiled broadly and crossed the room to shake hands with his son-in-law and to kiss his daughter's cheek. "I'm very glad for you. It'll be good to have some youngsters around again. If we can help in any way, you only have to ask."

Fred again felt the familiar pang of sadness that his parents were not there to offer their congratulations too, but the moment passed. He was just happy to have such kind and loving parents-in-law.

Lizzie and Fred loved their new home, although they hadn't realised the extent of the work needed to clean and refresh it. The old woman apparently had dozens of paintings and portraits hanging on the walls, and now that they had been taken down, there were huge faded patches underneath. Everywhere seemed dusty and musty, and there was quite a bit of repair needed, but Lizzie optimistically declared that it was all possible in the fulness of time. "We must find someone to help you," Fred said. "After all, I'm sure we can afford some domestic aid now. I'm a man of property. I'm not the young lad living in a stable any more. I'm Fred Lee, husband, property owner, and soon-to-be father." Lizzie smiled at his proud announcement and agreed that it would be a good idea to look for some help.

In fact, the promised help arrived by the end of the week. Harriet had knocked on Lizzie's door on the Monday morning. "Bertie is pining for you," she said, "so I've brought him over to see you and"—her tone turned to one of questioning—"possibly leave him with you?"

"Oh dear," Lizzie responded, "I really don't think I can have him here yet, Mama. There's so much to do, and to tell the truth, I'm finding it a little hard to cope with it all. Fred suggested we hire some domestic help, but I just haven't had the time to ask around."

Harriet, sensing that her daughter was near to tears, urged her to sit down and rest for a while. "I have an idea. I'm going out now, but I'll be back within the hour. Promise me you will stay there."

Lizzie nodded. Harriet rose to her feet and let herself out of the house. She made her way as quickly as possible to the library, where she wrote out a message in large capital letters: DAILY HELP NEEDED. GOOD WAGES OFFERED. DO NOT MISS THIS OPPORTUNITY TO APPLY FOR THIS HAPPY AND SATISFYING PLACEMENT. ASK AT THE DESK FOR DETAILS. After arranging the matter with the front desk, she then pinned the notice on the board before making her way back to her daughter.

Two days later, Lizzie opened her door to an unexpected visitor in the shape of a young girl, probably no more than fifteen years old. "Good morning, madam," she said shyly. "I'm Sarah, and I've come about the job." Although Lizzie had been told about her mother's advertisement, she had very little expectation of there being any result. After all, the library was largely frequented by scholars and academics or gentry with time on their hands, certainly not by young and seemingly uneducated girls.

"Come in. This is rather unexpected. How did you hear of the position I am offering?"

"My mum's friend does the cleaning at the library," Sarah replied. "She saw the notice and told my mum, and, well, that's why I'm here." Lizzie found herself warming to Sarah and her frank approach. After a few more questions, she found herself offering the job to the youngster.

"I presume you live locally and can come in each day? I shall need you for six hours a day at first, but I am expecting a baby, so after the birth I should like you to be here for eight to ten hours a day. I can offer you a wage of two shillings a week, and your midday meal will be provided. You may have every other Sunday free and one week a year as a paid holiday. Would that suit you?"

"Oh yes, please, madam," came the eager reply. "I promise I'll be a good worker. Thanks ever so."

"One more thing," Lizzie said, smiling. "My name is Mrs Lee, and that is how you should address me in future."

Sarah did indeed prove to be a good worker. In no time, the house was clean and shining. Bertie came back to live with his mistress, and after a few suspicious sniffs, he decided to accept Sarah as his friend. The dingy living room walls were repainted by one of Sarah's brothers, whilst another came in once a week to tend the garden. Fred insisted on paying them both, although they protested that it was good experience for them in their chosen careers, one as a decorator and the other as a gardener.

As Lizzie's time to give birth grew nearer, she was relaxed and happy and fully prepared for the next chapter in her life.

Twenty-eight

Lizzie and her mother embarked on a positive storm of sewing and knitting for the new baby. "Don't forget," warned Harriet, "the baby will be born in the summer, so you will only need light clothes for a while. Then we shall have to make everything in a bigger size for the winter." She had also started on an elaborate christening robe with pin tucks and lace, and with tiny pearl buttons for fasteners. Lizzie admitted she was not as accomplished as her mother and would stick to simpler knitting and sewing. In no time, bootees, mittens, and little vests began to pile up, together with a number of crocheted blankets. In March, Fred took a day off work and hired a horse and carriage to take them into Southampton. This was where the big stores were to be found. They intended to buy a cradle and one of the new perambulators.

"This is so exciting," enthused Lizzie, whilst hanging on to Fred's arm and looking up at him. "I can't wait to meet our little one. We shall have to think of some names before long, won't we?"

"If it's a boy, I should like him to have Frederick somewhere in his name," said Fred quietly, "after my pa, and me, of course."

And so, on 29 July 1889, when their little boy came into the world, he was named Joshua Frederick. Early that morning, Lizzie had sent Sarah to bring the midwife to her house because, as she informed Fred, "Things are beginning to happen." Harriet was also summoned and arrived in a very short while, bringing with her a welcome calming influence. Poor Fred was dismissed and told not to return until told to do so, which left him in two minds. Secretly he was relieved to be away from all the hustle and bustle, but on the other hand he wanted to be with his beloved wife at this very important time in their lives.

Everything went smoothly, giving the midwife cause to declare, "I wish all my new mothers were like you, Mrs Lee," as she wrapped the baby in a blanket and put him in his mother's arms. Joshua was already making his presence known by screwing up his little face and bawling. "He's got a strong pair of lungs," the midwife continued with a smile, "and he's a good weight, over seven pounds. Now, dear, I'm sure you want someone to find your husband."

Sarah was duly despatched, and in a very short while Fred came rushing into the room where Lizzie was propped up in bed holding their precious son. He felt the tears pouring down his face but didn't care, even if it was rather unmanly, because he was overwhelmed by love and the miracle of birth.

Josh, as he became known, was a delightful child with an intelligent mind. As he grew older, he was forever questioning the hows and whys of everything. He was fascinated by the motorcars which were beginning to be seen around the town, and when his father installed telephones at his business premises and at home, the boy's wonderment knew no bounds. "Please, may I telephone Uncle Richard?" he would implore. Usually Fred would acquiesce with a smile.

Fred had hoped that one day Josh would follow him into his construction company, but over the years it became obvious that his son was more interested in mechanics and engineering. When the Wright brothers flew their first aircraft, the lad announced, "That's what I'm going to do when I grow up! I'm going to be a pilot."

Fred and Lizzie smiled benignly at this outrageous idea. "And you'll fly to the moon, will you?"

Joshua did not remain an only child for long as his little sister Mary Ann Elizabeth was born just fifteen months later, followed at roughly two-year intervals by Ada Harriet, Susan Matilda, and

Martha Jane. Fred loved to share the joke with his son: "We've got to stand up for ourselves, Josh. We're the only two men with five ladies all wanting to have their own way!" Secretly, however, he could not have been more proud of his family. The best times were when they were all together, just enjoying each other's company.

Twenty-nine

During those years, Dunbar Village finally became a reality, and now it was a thriving little community centred around the chapel, the school, and a grocery store. The occupants of the fifty houses were very appreciative of their good fortune and were happy to work hard at the factory to show their gratitude towards their benefactor. Other businesses in the area had taken note of the quality of the building work supplied by Hancock & Lee, and the company continued to be inundated with enquiries and orders. Richard and Fred were becoming very wealthy men, much to their astonishment.

"Who would have thought in the early days that we would be so successful now?" said Fred. "I could still have been making kitchen tables, but here we are, self-made pillars of the community." The last comment was made with a wry grin. Then he continued, saying, "It's been hard work, though, hasn't it? I'm not young any more, and I'm beginning to feel a little weary of it all. And you, Richard, you are older than me. How do you feel?"

Richard nodded his head in agreement. "Yes, I've been thinking along the same lines, but I didn't want you to think that I was shirking or letting you down. I suppose the next step will be for us to find an efficient manager to take over some of the load." Fred agreed, saying he would make enquiries and maybe put an advertisement in the newspaper.

As their family expanded, Fred and Lizzie agreed that their first home was much too small for them all to live in comfortably. In fact, after Mary Ann's birth, Sarah had moved in permanently, becoming an indispensable and much-valued friend. She and Lizzie scoured the advertisements and billboards at one of the newly opened estate agents in the town, and within a few weeks they had found a house that was "just perfect" according to Lizzie. Situated in a village a few miles from Southampton, Summer Lodge consisted of six bedrooms, three of which had a small bathroom attached; a main bathroom; a spacious dining room; an impressive kitchen; and a parlour with tall windows overlooking a well-stocked garden.

Not only did the Lees now have a new home, but also they had the space for a couple of horses to be stabled, plus a trap big enough for the seven of them to take trips around the area, the New Forest and the River Hamble being among their favourites. Fred admitted he was growing too old to ride a bicycle now, saying the horses would be very useful "for the time being". Josh picked up on his father's rather enigmatic expression and, with excitement lighting up his eyes, said, "Do you mean that one day you might buy a motorcar?"

Fred laughed and agreed that maybe one day he would consider the idea, but not now. "Motorcars are a very new invention, and the whole thing might come to nothing in the end. They are noisy and unreliable. I can't see many people wanting to own one."

From the age of ten, Josh was a weekly boarder at Winchester College. Early every Monday morning, he and Fred would take the horse and trap to the station, where Josh would board the train to Winchester, and every Friday evening Fred would do the same journey in reverse. Josh enjoyed the camaraderie of his fellow pupils, even if they teased him about having four sisters, and he showed how tough he could be when he joined the rugby team, relishing the rough-and-tumble of the game. He studied hard at the subjects which interested him but admitted that Latin and Greek were quite beyond him.

Lizzie was determined that her daughters should have a good education. To her relief, she found a school just two miles away which had a very good reputation. Apart from learning the social skills of playing the piano, singing, and embroidering, the students were also taught arithmetic, geography, history, English grammar and literature, and the rudiments of French. The sisters had very different characters. Mary Ann was quite assertive and the one most likely to argue, whilst Ada was a dreamer. From her first few weeks at school, it was acknowledged that Susan was the "clever one", and the youngest sibling, Martha, was a born homemaker whose only ambition was to marry and raise a family. She was given a beautiful china doll on her third birthday and carried it around with her wherever she went, protesting loudly when she started school and had to leave Dolly at home.

Thirty

Having shared his thoughts with Richard about finding a manager for the company, Fred set about finding a suitable candidate. He had guessed this would not be an easy task, but still he could not help feeling rather despondent when time went by with no result. There was no shortage of men applying for the job, but Fred, much to his chagrin, found that in one way or another, not one of them was suitable. A month went by, then another and another, and still no one met his exacting standards. "It looks as if we shall have to carry on until we drop dead," he half-joked to Richard.

"Don't say that" was the reassuring reply. "Someone will turn up eventually."

"I wish I had your optimism," answered Fred. "I do sometimes wish that Josh or one of your sons would have been interested in joining our business, but it wasn't to be, was it?"

As it turned out, Richard's prediction was absolutely correct. A week later, a young man of about thirty years of age knocked on Fred's office door and announced that he was Stanley Jefferson from New Zealand. Fred's attention was immediately taken by the mention of New Zealand as he offered his visitor a seat. "What can I do for you?" he asked, fully expecting a request for a quotation or a contract for a new job.

"May I start at the beginning, sir? As I said, I'm from New Zealand, but I came over to England two years ago. It was intended to be just a brief visit, but I met a lovely young lady whom I married last year, and now I'm applying for English citizenship. The reason for my visit was that back in 1877, my father's sister, my aunt Kathleen, was returning home to Wanganui after six months in Europe and she lost her life in the *Avalanche* disaster. There were others from the same town who also drowned, and donations were sent in their memory towards the building of the Avalanche Church near Portland Bill. I was intrigued to see the church for myself."

Fred listened to the young man's explanation in silence, occasionally nodding his head, and at last exclaiming, "I too lost my family on that terrible night, as you probably know if you visited the church and saw the brass plaque there."

"Yes, indeed," agreed Stanley, "and then, quite by chance, I picked up an old newspaper yesterday and saw your advertisement for a manager. The newspaper was more than a month old, so I don't suppose the position is still open, but anyway, I thought there was no harm in asking, so here I am."

"No, we haven't employed anyone yet," Fred said slowly, "but if you are interested, you will have to show me your credentials and evidence of previous jobs, plus provide a reference. Shall we make an appointment for you to return here for a formal appointment with me and my partner, Richard Hancock?"

Stanley Jefferson passed the interview with flying colours. He already had a job managing a small company in Portsmouth, but he was eager to spread his wings. He answered every one of Fred's searching questions with intelligence and wisdom, which greatly impressed his prospective employers, although neither of them allowed a flicker of approval to show on their faces. Stanley even showed he had a good understanding of the financial side of a business which both Fred and Richard had always found to be a little difficult.

Finally, having discussed his salary, they shook hands on a mutually acceptable deal.

"I told you so!" said Richard triumphantly when their new manager had left the office. "Stanley Jefferson seems to be all that we had hoped for. I knew someone would come along eventually." Fred could only agree wholeheartedly with a relieved smile stretching from ear to ear.

Thirty-one

Contrary to Fred's gloomy predictions, motorcars were becoming more and more commonplace. Brooklands, the world's first purpose-built racing circuit, opened in 1907, and as an eighteenth birthday treat for Joshua, the father and son spent an enthralling couple of days there, staying overnight in a small boardinghouse in a nearby village. Fred was at last forced to acknowledge that motorcars were here to stay, and he promised his excited son that he would look into the matter of acquiring one.

True to his word, catalogues began to appear in the post, and by the end of the year Fred became the proud owner of a large family car in which seven people could squeeze themselves, albeit somewhat uncomfortably.

Joshua left Winchester College with a creditable number of exam passes. His ambitions still lay in aviation, but he acknowledged that it was far too early for him to think of this in terms of a career. He was absolutely certain that in a very few years aeroplanes would be flying commercially and maybe even socially. It was such an exciting prospect. He told himself that he would just be patient until the time came.

He filled his days doing a variety of unskilled jobs, finding no satisfaction in any of them, and then he heard about the newly opened flying school at Brooklands. Having applied for a place and waited on tenterhooks for an answer he was ecstatic when, two weeks later, Josh received a letter confirming that his application had been successful.

In his excitement, he naively expected to be flying within a very short time and was somewhat deflated to discover that the first six months were to be devoted entirely to technical instruction, the messy business of servicing the engine, and becoming familiar with every single part of the aircraft without ever leaving the ground. However, the great day finally arrived when he and his instructor stumbled into the skies in a rickety biplane and stayed aloft for a whole fifteen minutes. Not long after that, Josh celebrated his twenty-first birthday by flying solo at a speed of sixty miles an hour. "Would you believe that?" he exclaimed to his incredulous sisters. "That's almost as fast as an express train!"

In the meantime, as each of the four sisters attained the age of fifteen, they left school to pursue their adult lives. Mary Ann immersed herself in the suffragette movement, although she never actually took part in any of the demonstrations or hunger strikes. She totally admired women like Emmeline Pankhurst who regularly suffered so much in their effort to gain the vote for women, but she admitted that she was too young herself and did not have the inner strength for that sort of work. Instead, she arranged for the printing and distribution of thousands of leaflets proclaiming, "Deeds, not words", and phrases such as her idol had used at one of her trials: "We are not here as lawbreakers, but in an effort to become lawmakers." On one occasion, Mary Ann bravely carried a placard around the town of Southampton, but she was so disturbed by the open hostility and insults thrown at her that it was a long time before she attempted to do so again.

Ada had a much quieter personality. She had a talent for music, not only playing the piano very well, but also learning the intricacies of the violin, which she had received from her parents on the day that she left school. The highlight of her week was when her music tutor came for a precious two hours to pass on his knowledge and skill to his eager pupil. At the end of the session, teacher and student would sit on the long piano stool playing and singing together, to their great enjoyment. Ada had the quiet ambition that one day she would be good enough to play at the Great Hall in Southampton or even further afield.

Susan was the acknowledged clever one as stated earlier. She had left school that summer and had been accepted to study at Southampton University when she reached the age of eighteen. She was determined to become a doctor one day and intended to use the next two or three years reading and gaining as much knowledge as she possibly could in her chosen subjects of science and medicine.

As for Martha, she described herself as an "unambitious homemaker" and was quite content helping her mother and Sarah in all things domestic. It gave her pleasure to see the furniture gleaming after a vigorous application of elbow grease and beeswax. One day Sarah asked Lizzie if she could have a word with her. Upon agreeing, Lizzie was astounded to hear that her faithful housekeeper was planning to be married and would be moving away from the district.

"I had no idea you were courting!" she exclaimed.

"It's all rather sudden," Sarah responded bashfully. "My Rob is a widower of four years' standing, and he wants to settle down again. It's not just a convenience for him, you know. He really loves me, and I love him."

"I'm very happy for you, my dear," Lizzie replied. "You will make a splendid wife, and I'm sure you will be very happy together." She ruefully added, "But I will miss you so much, not just for your hard work, but also for your friendship over all these years. Still, the children are all grown up now, and Martha is a great help, so I'm sure we will manage. You will invite us to the wedding, won't you?"

"It's going to be a very quiet affair," Sarah replied, "but of course, you will be our honoured guests."

Having optimistically assumed that Martha would be there to help on the domestic front, Lizzie could have had no idea of the events about to unfold. Over the years, Fred's attitude towards the church had mellowed somewhat, although he and Lizzie had never been constant churchgoers, only attending at Christmas and Easter and a few occasions throughout the year. Their family had followed suit except for Martha, who went along every Sunday, rain or shine, and eventually became a Sunday school teacher. She loved the little ones and had a talent for bringing alive the stories from the Bible, so they all sat quietly, enthralled and eager to ask questions at the end. Harvest Festival was a special time when the children looked forward to taking their gifts into "the big church". On one such occasion, a young curate by the name of Frank Cowper was visiting. Martha took one look at him and, as she admitted later, knew he was the one for her right from that moment. For his part, Frank confessed to the same feelings. He rather shyly approached Martha after the service in the hope that she would at least pass the time of day with him and was delighted when she responded positively.

In a few short weeks, Frank and Martha became engaged. On the one hand, her parents were happy for their youngest daughter, but on the other, they were most alarmed that Frank appeared to be penniless. Granted, he had now been offered a position at a small church on the outskirts of Portsmouth, but his stipend was minimal, to say the least. "We will manage," Martha assured her parents. "After all, Frank has already been offered a small cottage which belongs to the parish, and I can help with the paperwork and maybe even find some work in the village."

"And how will you manage when a family comes along?" demanded Lizzie.

"We will manage," Martha confidently replied.

Fred and Lizzie finally gave in to their daughter's insistence and agreed that the couple could marry, but not until Martha turned eighteen.

The young couple decided on a simple ceremony to be performed by Frank's old friend whom he had met at college. Frank's parents had tragically been killed ten years prior in a train crash in Cheshire, and the grief-stricken seventeen-year-old had left his home to live with his aunt and uncle in Dorking before going on to theological college. He had been warmly welcomed into the family and had become great friends with his cousin Isaac, who was now about to be his best man. Martha chose to walk down the aisle with both her mother and her father in a sentimental digression from common practice, which everyone agreed was a lovely thought. Her parents couldn't have been more proud of their young daughter, and Fred admitted to a certain wetness around the eyes as he saw Frank lovingly take Martha's hand to lead her towards the altar.

In April 1912, the Royal Mail Steamer *Titanic* left Southampton Docks bound for the United States, and many of Fred's friends and neighbours travelled down to the docks to witness this historic event. The *Titanic* was the largest passenger ship ever built, operated by the White Star Line and heralded as being "luxurious" and "unsinkable". When the unbelievable news came through that she had struck an iceberg in the middle of the Atlantic and sunk within a short time, Fred was utterly horrified. Memories of his own dreadful experience came flooding back, and that night he suffered a vivid nightmare in which he too was struggling in the icy water before succumbing to the cold. As he gasped and thrashed around in bed, Lizzie instinctively understood the agonies going through her husband's mind. She gently woke him, and they talked quietly until morning came and Fred had recovered his senses. Nevertheless, his grief was very near the surface for many days to follow.

Thirty-two

Not long after the happiness of Martha's wedding day, the world was about to change as a disastrous war broke out across Europe. In June 1914, Archduke Franz Ferdinand, heir to the Austro-Hungarian empire, was assassinated in Sarajevo by a nineteen-year-old Bosnian Serb activist. This seemingly irrelevant occurrence stirred up a maelstrom of bitterness and hatred between the great nations of Europe, and ordinary citizens were horrified when war was declared just two months later. The optimists said it would all be over by Christmas, but in fact it dragged on for four terrible years, in which millions of people lost their lives.

As a clergyman, Frank was exempt from service, but Joshua, having fulfilled his dream of becoming a pilot, was immediately conscripted into the battle zone, flying his flimsy little aircraft over enemy territory accompanied by his navigator and a gunner in the rear. He wrote home as often as possible, sending heavily censored letters to his parents assuring them that he was well. Fred and Lizzie were extremely proud of him, of course, but this was tinged with absolute terror that their precious son might come to harm. Six months before the conflict came to an end in November 1918, Joshua's letters did indeed cease to arrive. At first Fred and Lizzie refused to accept the awful fact that he might not have survived, but all their enquiries came to nothing. Finally they had to accept the fact with devastating sorrow that he had probably been killed. The family were desolate, as were so many other people who had lost their loved ones. They felt beaten down by their emotions, but gradually, as the weeks went slowly by, they arrived at an unwilling acceptance that Joshua had died a hero's death serving his country. They were extremely proud of him.

Imagine their incredulous joy, therefore, when one cool October day there was a knock at the door, which was opened to reveal a beaming Josh standing on the doorstep. Lizzie felt momentarily faint in her relief, whilst Fred stepped forward and hugged his son as if he would never let him go.

"There's a fire burning in the sitting room," said Lizzie when she had recovered a little. "Go and sit in there and warm yourself up while I get you a cup of tea."

"Tea!" Fred laughed. "Surely this calls for champagne!"

But Josh nodded at his mother. "A cup of good old English tea would be wonderful." At that moment Joshua's sisters appeared in the hallway, wondering what all the excited clamour was about, and as one they rushed over to their brother to hug and kiss him and exclaim about his miraculous return.

Josh laughingly held up his hands. "Let's go into the sitting room, and I will tell you all about the last few months." With his hands cupping his welcome hot drink, he began his narrative.

"We were incredibly lucky for the first three years or so, managing to return home more or less in one piece every time we flew over to the Continent on a raid. It's rather dreadful to admit now, but there was great exhilaration every time we managed to shoot down an enemy plane. One tended to forget in the heat of battle that they were someone's son or someone's husband. Anyway, the last sortie we were involved in was to be our last because we were shot down into the English Channel."

Lizzie gasped loudly at this and put her hand to her mouth in horror. "Sorry, my dear, do please continue," she said once she had composed herself.

"Well, there I was bobbing about in the water, and I can tell you it was dashed cold. There was no sign of my navigator or my gunner, and very sadly I concluded that they must have been killed by the bullets which hit our plane. I don't remember how long I was in the water, but I managed to stay afloat, and by God's good grace I was spotted by a small fishing boat and taken ashore in Belgium, where I was transferred to a hospital. I had lost my dog tag, and when they asked me my name, to my utter consternation I couldn't remember. In fact, I had absolutely no idea about my life at all; details of where I came from or if I had a family were all a complete blank. In the meantime, of course, I had been listed as missing, presumed dead, although I believe that for some reason you never received the message."

The family all stared round-eyed at Josh, but before they could ask any questions, he started speaking again. "I must have hit my head on something, or perhaps when I dropped into the freezing Channel the shock did something to my brain. The hospital staff were so kind and patient with me. I think they regarded me as something of a novelty! Whenever the nurses could spare the time, they would sit by me and try to get me to remember something, but there was nothing for a long time apart from the fact that I spoke English. Then I started to have dreams, nightmares actually, and gradually I began to piece things together. When I finally recalled my name and my home address, arrangements were made for me to be returned to England. So here I am." He said this last bit with a flourish.

His speechless family stared at him for many moments before all beginning to speak at once.

"My dear boy, thank goodness you're safe now," one said.

"You're a hero, and we're so proud of you," said another.

"How did you feel when you were in such danger?" one asked.

"Will you have to go back?" Lizzie asked fearfully.

"Not in a fighting capacity," Josh replied. "I've been invalided out of the service, and in any case all the signs are there that this terrible war will come to an end soon. Then I hope to become a civilian pilot transporting goods, and maybe people, around the world, but first, of course, I'll have to prove that I'm absolutely fit again because it's such a responsible task. If I can't do that, then I'll have to settle for a ground job. But one thing is definite, and that is that I want to stay with the aviation services.

"There's one other thing I haven't told you about yet," said Josh with a twinkle in his eyes. "There were so many wonderful people in the hospital who literally helped me back from the brink of despair, but there was one in particular called Anique. She was so gentle and patient with me, and, well, to tell the truth, before I left, I asked her to marry me." He finished the sentence in a rush of words.

"And did she say yes?" Lizzie asked rather breathlessly.

"She did indeed!" Josh happily replied. "She will join me when she can, but she must stay at the hospital until the war ends because Belgium, although it declared neutrality at the beginning of the war, is supposedly under German occupation. I say 'supposedly' because the German forces more or less retreated from her home town many months ago, and their presence now is almost nonexistent. In fact, I never came across one German the whole time I was in hospital. And there was no opposition to my leaving Belgium to return home, although officially, I suppose, I was a prisoner of war. I can't wait to see her again. I'm sure you will love her as much as I do. And by the way, you may be relieved to know that she speaks good English with just the quaintest of accents."

The fire had long burned down to ashes, and the cups of tea had been emptied, but still the family sat comfortably and in great harmony. At Josh's announcement, the questions started again.

"What does she look like?" one asked.

"Does she have brothers and sisters?" another queried.

"Are her parents still alive and living in Belgium?" another asked.

"Do you think she will continue with her nursing?"

Finally Lizzie interrupted. "Hush, hush, everyone. I'm sure Josh will tell us all about her in due course, but for now he looks tired and must be in need of a rest. I shall go and prepare supper. And yes, Fred, I think we should open a bottle of champagne. This has been the most amazing and wonderful day, and our hearts and minds are overflowing with gratitude, Josh, that you should be back at home with us, safe and sound and happy." She rose from her chair. "Ever since you enlisted, your room has been cleaned but otherwise left untouched. Your bed is ready for you, and your wardrobe is full of your clothes."

"That's a relief." Josh grinned. "I lived in hospital pyjamas for weeks, but my uniform was cleaned and dried, so I did have something decent to wear on my journey home."

Ever the practical one, Mary Ann offered to go to the local post office to send a telegram to Martha. "She will be over the moon to hear the news. Maybe she and Frank will come to visit us, although she may find the journey too much of a strain because, Josh, you don't know this, you are about to become an uncle."

"How exciting! Tell her then that I will travel to Portsmouth in a day or so when I have caught up on my sleep and eaten some of Mother's delicious food."

In November 1918, church bells rang out across the land in thanksgiving that the war was finally at an end and Europe was at peace again, albeit at such a terribly grim cost. Christmas in the Lee household that year was an enormous celebration that seemed to go on for days. Anique arrived from Belgium in time to join the festivities, whilst Martha, Frank, and the new baby, Alice, travelled over from Portsmouth once Frank had performed his parochial duties on Christmas Day. They all laughed, sang, played silly games, and ate delicious meals, but most of all they were deeply thankful that they could enjoy each other's company once again.

Thirty-three

Four months later, Anique's parents arrived from Belgium in preparation for the wedding, having accepted Harriet and John's invitation to stay with them. The two couples hit it off from their first meeting. They found it easier to converse in French, and although none of them was expert, they managed to understand one another very well. And Anique was there, of course, to translate if they really got into difficulty.

The date was set for the beginning of May. Anique happily announced that sisters and brothers, uncles and aunts, cousins and friends, had all been invited and would be staying at a local hotel. Josh, on the other hand, had kept his invitees to his immediate family and a few old friends. To avoid any possible ill feeling among her many relatives, Anique had asked a friend from the hospital to be her only bridesmaid, whilst Josh had enlisted Richard's son, Henry, to support him as best man.

The day was fine and dry, and the bride looked beautiful in her simple white sheath gown, which daringly showed her ankles. She and her bridesmaid carried enormous bouquets of spring flowers, whilst Josh was rather dapper in a morning suit and top hat. The photographer painstakingly took many pictures of the bride and groom, of their parents, of their attendants, and of their guests, until Josh tactfully said, "I think we have enough now. Thank you so much."

At the reception held in a local hall, he noticed and was concerned that one of his friends looked very ill and had a bad cough. "You all right, Charlie?" he enquired.

He was answered with a gruff, "Yes, thanks."

Three days later Lizzie complained of a bad headache and said she felt shivery and rather unwell, concluding that she would go to bed for a while. During the night, Fred awoke to find her glistening with perspiration, breathing heavily, and coughing a dry cough, which made her throat rasp. A terrible fear engulfed him that she might have contracted the dreaded Spanish flu which was sweeping the world. He had read about it in the newspapers and knew that many millions of people had already died. He groaned loudly, which aroused Lizzie from a fitful sleep.

"Do you think I've picked up that awful Spanish flu?" she asked weakly. Fred could only nod. He tried to remain calm for his darling wife's sake, but inside he was panic-stricken because he knew there was no cure and Lizzie would have to battle it out on her own.

"We'll call the doctor first thing in the morning," he said. She nodded, although they both knew there was very little the doctor could do for her.

The mood of the whole household changed from one of happily remembering the wedding to one of extreme concern for Lizzie. The family decided not to tell Joshua, who was now away on his honeymoon. He would be told as soon as he returned home, of course, and would no doubt remember how ill his friend Charlie had looked at the wedding. He would probably come to the sad conclusion, as had the rest of the family, that his mother had caught the fever from his friend. Nobody knew at that time whether or not Charlie had survived, but they all sincerely hoped that he had recovered.

Mary Ann, Ada, and Susan made up a rota of care. They ordered a supply of masks to be worn when they were in Lizzie's bedroom, and they insisted that Fred should rest as much as possible. Day and night for nearly a week someone was always there tending to Lizzie, wiping the sweat from her body, and giving her regular sips of water. They held her hand and whispered words of encouragement. Slowly, the fever began to subside until Lizzie was finally able to sit up in bed and enjoy a nourishing bowl of soup. Fred wept copious tears in his relief. Although he had tried to hide his despair from the family, in private he had been utterly distraught.

Lizzie was still very weak and had lost a lot of weight, but she was so very glad that she was still alive. She was able to sit in the garden in the warm sunshine, and although her appetite was small, she enjoyed the tasty dishes which her daughters provided for her. Slowly, her cheeks showed some colour and she became stronger, until at last she felt fit enough to invite one or two of her friends around for a cup of tea and to thank them for all the flowers and kind messages they had sent.

Josh and Anique returned home and were horrified to learn of the near-calamity which had occurred whilst they were away. As predicted, Josh remembered his friend and determined to find out what had happened to him.

"I'm so very thankful," said Lizzie, "not only that have I survived, but also that no one else in our immediate circle caught the fever."

Thirty-four

Fred had found it impossible to work whilst Lizzie was so ill. He knew he would not be able to concentrate and might make some serious mistakes, so Richard had promised to see to everything. However, Fred's absence from work brought to mind his conversation with Richard some time before when they both had acknowledged that it might be time to retire. "After all," Richard said, "we're not getting any younger, and we have a very reliable manager in Stanley. Let's give it some serious thought. Perhaps we could make an appearance at work on random days—keep the workforce on their toes!"

Fred laughed and agreed. That evening when he arrived home, he said to Lizzie, "I've got something I want to discuss with you. Come and sit down."

However, she insisted that first of all he should eat the tasty supper she had prepared. "Whatever you want to talk about, it can wait just a little bit longer." An hour later, when they were sitting comfortably in their armchairs, she said, "Well then, Fred! What is it?"

Fred slowly began to recount his conversation with Richard. "And when you were so ill," he continued, "I realised how very much I wanted to spend more time with you and the family. You've been so patient over the years, never complaining about the time I spent with the business trying to make it a success and to make a name for myself. What do you think? Don't decide now. Just think it over. But could you possibly bear to have me around the house most of the day, getting in your way and messing up your plans?" The last was said with an enquiring but rather concerned look on his face because he was well aware that Lizzie had a good circle of friends and many interests.

However, the anxious moment immediately vanished as Lizzie crossed over to him, kissed the top of his head, and reassured him that she would like nothing better, saying that it would make her very happy to have his company all day, every day. "I think it's a marvellous idea," she enthused. "At last we'll have some time to indulge ourselves. We can go to visit Josh and his family, as well as Martha and her brood, or we can go out somewhere in the car. Perhaps we can even take a holiday. Or go to the theatre together. That would be wonderful!"

"Yes, all in good time," Fred replied, slightly amused, as he thought how very good it was to see the old sparkle and energy coming back to his beloved wife.

Once his working life became less pressurised, Fred began to develop a few hobbies. He discovered a passion for gardening, and he and Lizzie spent many happy hours together planting and weeding. Under their industrious hands, a colourful display of flowers bloomed from March to October. Even during the winter months, there was plenty to occupy them, such as pruning, potting, and preparing for the spring. To his surprise, Fred also developed a liking for books, and he was often to be found sitting back in his armchair engrossed in a novel. He had also always loved to sing but lacked the nerve to do so in public until he discovered a local men's choir, and now that he could spare the time, he joined them every Tuesday evening, singing his heart out in very convivial company.

Fred had always taken an interest in Dunbar Village and its inhabitants. Before he retired, he would occasionally find the time to make a visit, chatting to the residents and asking if they had any problems with their housing. Apart from the odd minor fault, he was always gratified to learn that they were very happy. He now thought guiltily that it had been a long time since his last visit; in fact, looking back, he figured it must have been before the war. He hastened to rectify the situation by driving to the village the following week when Lizzie was enjoying lunch with some friends.

Once there, Fred was struck immediately by the downbeat atmosphere. There were no groups of cheerful women chatting to one another and no children playing. In fact, there was hardly anyone about. He called to one older woman who was hanging out what seemed to be an enormous amount of washing, "Good morning, Mrs Harris. Where is everyone today?"

"Ah, good morning, sir," she replied. "Most of the women are working in the factory now, and the children who are old enough have jobs too." Noting Fred's puzzled expression, she continued, "You see, sir, our men all went to serve during the war, and only one or two came home. It was a tragedy beyond reasoning that so many of our fine young men were lost. The rest of us women have had to pull together and earn what we can to keep our families together." Indicating the line of washing, she gave a wry smile. "This is my contribution. On a wet day it can be really unpleasant!"

Fred felt stunned by this account of such stoicism. There he and Lizzie were planning a future of self-indulgence and pleasure, whilst the lives of these poor women had been shattered. He berated himself for having given so little thought to them and promised himself he would try to make amends in some way. That evening he discussed the problem with Lizzie. For hours it seemed that one of them would present an idea only for the other to find difficulties with it. They were about to give up when Fred's glance fell upon a photograph of Josh as a schoolboy.

"I have it!" exclaimed Fred. "I think it might be possible to set up some sort of trust for the children at Dunbar Village whereby all their education would be free and they, or their mothers, would be paid a certain sum to compensate for their loss of earnings. It seems dreadful to me that those bright young minds are being wasted on some menial job when their futures could be so promising. That's just a rough idea which will need to be sorted out professionally, and of course it won't apply to everyone."

Lizzie nodded thoughtfully. "That sounds a huge undertaking, my dear. Do you really think it's possible?"

"I hope so," he replied. "And do you know, Lizzie, I'd like to think of it as expressing my tremendous gratitude towards some Fate, or God, or whatever that led to Lucky's and my decision to stay in England all those years ago. Was there some unfathomable reason why I was allowed to live? some expectation for me to do well, perhaps? some reparation I was to make?"

After many weeks of complicated legal work and many hours of discussions, the Frederick Lee Trust was finally set up officially. There were several clauses and provisos, but essentially it meant that the benefits would apply to the war widows and their children on the understanding that said benefits would cease when the child finished his education or up to a limit of twelve years. The careworn mothers were finally able to relax a little, and Fred's belief that there could be many talented Dunbar children proved to be correct. In fact, in the coming years, thanks to the generosity of their benefactor, there were to be many teachers, doctors, and lawyers joining the professional ranks. In the fulness of time, of course, the bereaved children would become adults and the trust would come to an end, but for the time being Fred felt a certain easing of his prickly conscience.

Thirty-five

It was a very cold day towards the middle of January 1922. Fred was sitting in his favourite armchair reading the newspaper. Lizzie was companionably sitting opposite, busily knitting a blanket for Josh and Anique's second child.

"It says here that Ernest Shackleton has died," Fred said. "That's sad news, isn't it? Do you remember when he went on that fateful expedition to the Antarctic in—I'm not sure. Was it 1916 when his ship got trapped in the ice and eventually sank and all his men had to live for months on the floating ice?"

"Yes. I remember that," Lizzie replied, "and then later on they set off in small boats and eventually reached a whaling station. And the miracle was that no one died."

"Such brave men. What they endured doesn't bear thinking about. It's cold here today, but just think what it would be like existing in temperatures of minus fifty degrees." They smiled at one another as they regarded the blazing fire in the hearth and thought of how fortunate they were.

Their conversation drifted to an entirely different subject, that of Ada's forthcoming marriage. After years of sitting side by side at the piano, Ada and her music tutor had suddenly realised that they were very much in love and wanted to spend the rest of their lives together. Alfred had plucked up the courage to approach Fred and was only able to relax when Fred granted his permission and smiled, the two men shaking hands with Fred wishing Alfred a happy life.

Ada had already advised her mother what was going on in the sitting room. Whilst Lizzie was delighted by her daughter's obvious happiness, she felt she just had to voice a small concern: "Alfred is fifteen years older than you, my dear. He will be a fairly old man when you will still be comparatively young."

"I know," Ada replied, "but it makes no difference to our feelings, and I'm certain that he will take care of me as I will take care of him." As they rejoined the men, Alfred had crossed over from the fireplace, where he had been standing, to put his arm round his new fiancée's waist, whilst Ada gave him a swift kiss on the cheek.

Some days later, the couple again approached Fred and Lizzie. "Please don't be upset by what I'm going to tell you, but we have both decided we don't want a church wedding. We plan to be married quite soon in a registry office in London with just a handful of guests. That will be both of you, of course, Alfred's widowed mother, and any of my sisters who can get away for the day. We're fairly certain that Josh and Anique won't be able to travel all the way to London because the new baby is due soon, but naturally they will receive an invitation."

Fred, sensing Lizzie's faint disapproval, tried to make a joke to ease the tension. "Well, that will save me spending my money on some extravagant affair. Seriously, the decision lies with both of you, and if you're happy to marry in a registry office, then so be it."

"There's something else," said Ada, biting her lip. "Soon after we are married, we are going to live in France. Alfred has been offered a prestigious post at the Paris Conservatoire and is eager to take it up."

Lizzie gasped at this piece of news and couldn't help blurting out, "But that's so far away, Ada! You will be all alone when Alfred is working."

"I know," she replied, "but thanks to your insistence that me and my sisters get a good education, I am able to speak quite passable French, and I very much hope that I'll be able to make some friends in due time. Of course, I—we—will miss you all terribly, but Paris isn't so far away, and I believe the telephone lines are reasonably good nowadays." Trying to lighten the atmosphere, she added jokingly, "You might even be able to fly over in one of the new passenger aircraft!"

Lizzie inwardly shuddered but remained silent, just hugging her daughter tightly to her side.

In March of that same year, Fred and Lizzie boarded the train from Southampton to Waterloo. They proceeded from there to the small hotel in Victoria where they had spent their honeymoon so many years before and were greeted by a man bordering on middle age who seemed faintly familiar. "Forgive me," questioned Lizzie, "but are you the young lad who used to run errands and earn pocket tips for your trouble? I believe his name was Harry."

"I am indeed Harry. At your service, Mr and Mrs Lee," he replied with a laugh. "I must have been insufferable in those days, but I am now the proprietor of this grand establishment. When I reached the age of twenty-one, my parents took retirement and are at present enjoying themselves on permanent holiday somewhere in Cornwall." Again with a broad smile, he said, "I will call my ten-year-old son Teddie to show you to your room and carry your luggage. No doubt he will be grateful for a small tip!" They all laughed and agreed that some things never seemed to change.

For her wedding, Ada had chosen a simple calf-length white silk dress. Small silver-coloured tassels danced around the hem, whilst her neck was adorned by a long string of pearls, which was Alfred's present to his bride. On her head was a small cloche hat which fitted closely over her recently cropped hair, and in her hand she carried a single red rose. Lizzie was very proud of her beautiful daughter despite the fact that she could not bring herself to wholly approve of Ada's haute couture outfit. She admonished herself that she should really try to move with the times, but she couldn't ever see herself showing so much leg in public.

Mary Ann also attended the wedding. After the brief ceremony and the obligatory photographic session, the five of them, together with Alfred's mother, made their way by cab to Rules Restaurant for a celebratory meal. Fred had chosen this venue as a fond reminder to his wife of their first day on honeymoon in London. Now he announced buoyantly, "Choose just what you would like to eat. It's the least I can do for you two lovely people, even if it does cost an arm and a leg.

"I'm only joking," he added swiftly as his daughter looked at him with some concern. "I mean it! Let's enjoy every minute of this very special day."

Everyone scanned the menu and made their individual choices. Another waiter hovered near their table until Fred realised he was waiting to take their wine order. "I think we should order some champagne. What do you suggest?" Fred asked the waiter, trying not to show his ignorance of fine wines.

"I would recommend a bottle of Ayala, sir," the waiter responded. "It is a very fine wine and extremely popular at present." The Ayala duly arrived, nicely chilled and resting in an ice bucket. The waiter made a great show of uncorking the bottle before pouring a little into each glass.

"A toast!" Fred announced jovially, holding his glass high in the air. "To Ada and Alfred. May you enjoy a lifetime of happiness." They all raised their glasses to take a sip of this highly recommended wine.

Lizzie couldn't help but grimace at the taste. *I'm such a country bumpkin,* she thought with inward amusement. *This sophisticated life is obviously not for me.* She was aware that Fred was smiling at her, no doubt sharing her thoughts, and it seemed as if the rest of the party were none too impressed either. "Shall we order a jug of water as well?" she asked. The suggestion was met with some relief.

The afternoon passed only too quickly, and soon it was time to part company, Fred, Lizzie, and Mary Ann back to their hotel, Alfred's mother to her flat in Chelsea, and the newly married couple to Waterloo Station for their train to Dover, where they had booked a hotel for the night. The next day they would take the ferry across the English Channel and then a train to Nice for a brief honeymoon before Alfred took up his new post in Paris.

Lizzie found it difficult not to cry as she hugged her daughter goodbye. "You will write, won't you?" she asked, her voice breaking with emotion. "And I will write to you as often as I can."

"Please do," responded Ada. "I know I'm going to miss you all terribly. Tell me all the family news, and keep my piano tuned, won't you? I want it to make a good sound when we visit. And we will visit; you know that, don't you?"

Lizzie managed to smile at her daughter's obvious attempt to lighten the atmosphere, before blowing her a kiss and moving away.

Thirty-six

Back home, the rooms all seemed strangely silent. At first, Lizzie found it difficult to adjust. She was so accustomed to bustling about and tending to her family that often she found herself beginning to prepare a meal for five or six people before realising that it would be just her and Fred sitting down at the table that evening. Mary Ann spent every day in Southampton campaigning for the suffragette movement and often stayed overnight with a friend in order to make preparations for the next day, so Lizzie and Fred saw their daughter only occasionally at breakfast or supper. Susan, to her great pride and satisfaction, had gained a place at medical college and was away from home most of the time, just occasionally visiting at weekends. Even then she was immersed in her books and studying hard towards achieving the qualifications she would need to practise as a doctor.

On the days when the echoing silence of the once busy house was too much to bear, Lizzie would make the short journey into town and visit the library. Her father, now an old man, had sold the premises to the local authority many years before. It was now known as a public library. There was still the same dusty atmosphere about it, however, and she loved to sit quietly at one of the tables and watch everything going on around her.

Sometimes Josh and Anique and their two children would drop by as they lived nearby. Josh's career was doing very well. He was now the proud co-owner of a charter plane and much in demand flying all over Europe on various commissions. Lizzie loved those days when she could pamper her grandchildren and play games with them.

Less frequently, Martha, Frank, and their four children would arrive, sometimes to stay the night, and Lizzie was in her element. She adored all her grandchildren and looked forward to the time when there were even more. The downside of their visits was, of course, the emptiness that sometimes threatened to engulf her when they had returned to their own homes, but Fred always managed to lighten her mood and soon have her laughing again.

Although Fred had promised to retire, he still couldn't stop himself from occasionally dropping into the office, but now he had come to the definite and final decision that he would retire completely. "From now on I will devote my time to Lizzie. She has been so uncomplaining about the long hours I have worked, and it's time now to enjoy our days together." That evening, he announced his decision to Lizzie: "I'm not going into the works any more. Not at all. Not even for an hour. I am absolutely and definitely retired. You see before you a gentleman of leisure!"

Lizzie rewarded him with a radiant smile. "That's wonderful news! What shall we do tomorrow? Let's make some plans."

Fred laughed and said, "Tell me, Mrs Lee, what would you really like to do?"

Hardly pausing to reflect, Lizzie replied, "I think I should like to go to Paris. It's been nearly a year since Ada and Alfred were married and left for France, and although she has written lots of letters which are full of news, it would be really lovely to see them again."

Fred nodded his agreement. "That's a very good idea. I'll see about booking our tickets in a month's time if that's convenient for Ada."

"I'll write to her at once. She will be so surprised to hear that we're planning to visit her." Lizzie then turned to Fred and added with a laugh, "Just one thing, Fred. Don't expect me to travel to France in an aeroplane. I know Josh says they are entirely safe and are destined to be the transport of the future, but to me it seems totally against nature that people should fly through the air in such a heavy contraption."

Fred nodded in agreement, but added, "That's just what I said about motorcars, but just look how many of them are on the roads now and how convenient they are."

Thirty-seven

Exactly thirty days later, Fred and Lizzie left their home in the very early morning to take the train to Dover and then on to the port itself. Fred carried two small suitcases which contained, Lizzie hoped, enough clothing to last them for the whole of their stay. They arrived at the terminal clutching their passports, their tickets, and a purse full of francs to spend on their holiday and on treats for their daughter. It was the first time either of them had travelled abroad; mixed in with their excitement was a certain apprehension. How would they cope with the journey, with the customs office, and above all, with the language? They were fortunate in that the weather was fine and dry with only the slightest swell to the sea, and they found it exhilarating to stand on the deck with the breeze ruffling their hair as they watched the surge of water behind the bows of the ship. Lizzie admitted that she had really been quite worried, but now she found she was enjoying the experience very much indeed.

As the ship moved slowly into its mooring place, they could see an excited little figure waving from the dockside. "Look! There's Ada. How wonderful that she's come to meet us!" Fifteen minutes later they were hugging each other and exclaiming, "How well you look!" and "It's so good to see you."

"Let's go and retrieve your luggage," said Ada, "and then we'll go and find a cab to take us to the station."

The train journey to Paris took nearly three hours, but the time seemed to fly by as the beaming trio caught up with all their news.

It was dark when they finally arrived at the Gare du Nord and made their way to the small hotel just around the corner from the station. Ada suggested they have a light supper and then get a good night's sleep.

"I'm so sorry you can't come to our apartment," she said, "but there's only one bedroom, and the sitting room is quite cramped, so there's no room for a bed in there. However, it's not far away, so Alfred and I will be back tomorrow at ten o'clock." She paused before continuing. "And we shall have a surprise for you." With a somewhat enigmatic smile, she kissed her parents. "*Bonne nuit. Dors bien,*" she said, and departed.

Promptly at ten o'clock the next morning, Ada came into the hotel, followed by a smiling Alfred. "*Bonjour, mes cheres. Etes vous pret?*"

Lizzie laughed at her daughter, saying, "Enough, enough! You have shown us how well you can speak French, but please, for our sakes, may we talk in English now?"

Ada grinned and continued in English, saying, "And now I promised you a surprise, didn't I? Come outside and see what it is." She led the way to the roadside, where a gleaming Peugeot automobile was parked. "Well, what do you think? Alfred is on holiday this week, and it will be his pleasure to drive us around this beautiful city and show you the sights."

"Is it yours?" Lizzie gasped.

"I wish it were," Alfred responded, "but I've just borrowed it from a friend of mine at the Conservatoire who happens to be rather wealthy."

The next few days passed in a whirl of sightseeing with meals taken at little pavement cafes whenever they felt hungry. Lizzie was as excited as a young girl and would exclaim every few minutes at every new and interesting sight. Places she had only read about in her books were right there in front of her, and she felt like pinching herself to make sure that she, Elizabeth Lee, was actually in a foreign country, hearing foreign voices, and savouring the distinct aroma of the city, no doubt caused by the great number of people who were smoking rather pungent Gauloises cigarettes. Ada herself had taken up the habit, and her mother conceded that she looked very elegant waving her cigarette around in its long ivory holder. In fact, Ada had picked up a number of French idiosyncrasies in the past few months. For instance, it amused Lizzie to hear her daughter speaking fluent French whilst waving her hands about in typically Gallic fashion.

Alfred whisked them around his adopted city, pointing out various landmarks with some pride. "Over there is the Eiffel Tower. Do you know, it's a thousand feet high. We could take the lift to the top if you would like that." Lizzie, however, declined the offer, saying she would prefer to view the amazing sight from the river. So, they took a boat trip along the Seine. The next day, they visited Notre Dame Cathedral, and alongside there Lizzie discovered the famous Flower Market. She felt she could spend several hours drifting around the many colourful displays, but Ada was keen to move on to the Louvre, so Lizzie reluctantly took her leave.

"Le Louvre is enormous," Ada advised her parents. "You won't have time to see more than a few paintings, but I thought it would give you a thrill to stand in front of the *Mona Lisa*. Just imagine the stories you will be able to tell your friends when you return home!"

Day after day, more well-known landmarks were revealed. Lizzie was voluble in her enjoyment of it all, and Fred, though quieter, was just as impressed. All too soon, the last day of their holiday arrived. Ada suggested they should walk to the Arc de Triomphe and then browse among the fabulous shops on the Champs-Elysées.

"Don't expect me to buy anything," warned Lizzie. "I'm a little uncomfortable with modern fashion, and from what I've seen of the prices—well!"

Ada smiled at her. "You wear the clothes you are happy with, but I wager you'll be in shorter skirts too in a year or so. They are so liberating."

As they returned to the hotel, Ada turned to her parents and somewhat mysteriously said, "We have a surprise for you this evening. One last memory to take home. Alfred will meet you at seven o'clock, and we shall probably not return until midnight."

True to his word, Alfred arrived promptly. As they drove towards Montmartre, Fred spotted the famous Red Mill above a theatre door. "It's the Moulin Rouge!" he exclaimed. "An evening there will be a wonderful end to a wonderful week. Thank you both so much for thinking of it and for everything you've done to make it such a memorable holiday for both of us."

"Did you know that the original Moulin Rouge was destroyed by fire a few years ago?" asked Ada. "So, we're very lucky that it has reopened just in time for your visit."

Inside the building, the décor was resplendent: mirrored walls reflecting the sparkling chandeliers; seats covered in rich red velvet; and the occasional small table with a pristine white tablecloth scattered in. Attentive waiters hovered, and there was a great buzz of anticipation from the audience. Maurice Chevalier was among the entertainers that night. The crowd could hardly contain their excitement to see their hero come on to the stage to charm them all. The famous cancan dancers were also on the bill. Lizzie pretended to be scandalised by their high kicks and by glimpses of their frilly underwear. Beneath her long dress, however, her feet were tapping in time with the music, and she clapped enthusiastically along with the audience at the end of their energetic routine.

The day of departure dawned, and whilst Fred and Lizzie had enjoyed the most fabulous time, secretly they were both rather relieved that they were going home to enjoy Fred's retirement in a somewhat quieter way of life. They were sad to leave Ada and Alfred, but at the same time they had been reassured to see the young couple and had come to understand that they were very happy together. In fact, as Ada had forecast, they had both made some good friends and were very content with their life in France.

Ada, remember, had one more surprise for them. "I shall be returning across the Channel in a few months' time," she said, "because we want our child to be born in England." With a huge grin on her face, she waited for her parents' reaction and was rewarded by their open-mouthed astonishment.

"I never guessed," Lizzie managed to say, "but that's just wonderful news. Just imagine, Fred, another lovely grandchild!" She joyfully hugged and kissed her daughter.

Thirty-eight

Life felt rather flat for the first few days after Fred and Lizzie returned home. Mary Ann, who had been staying with a friend and her family, was due to come back in the next day or so, but in the meantime the house seemed empty and quiet. That all changed at the weekend, when Josh arrived with his family and the exciting news that they were expecting another baby. Lizzie was all smiles again and declared that she could never have enough grandchildren. She said that all of them had their individual characters and every one of them was precious to her.

At the same time, Mary Ann arrived home. The rather argumentative and determined Mary Ann the family had known all her life had almost disappeared, to be replaced by a much softer version who laughed a lot, sang out loud, and hummed tunes under her breath. Fred and Lizzie exchanged rather amused glances, and Lizzie whispered, "Do you think she's found a man?"

"That must be it," he replied.

They were proved right when Mary Ann confided in them on her second day at home. "I was on a protest march for the suffragettes, holding up my placard," she explained, "and usually all we get are jeers and verbal abuse from the men—and occasionally even from the women. However, this day a good-looking chap clapped his hands as we walked by and called out that he hoped we would succeed, that it was only fair for women to have the vote and he backed us all the way. It was so unexpected and so welcome that, I must admit, I gave him a big smile as we passed by. At the end of the march, there he was again, doffing his hat and asking if he could escort me home!" Mary Ann laughed at Lizzie's facial expression. "It is the twentieth century now, you know. And don't forget that your meeting with Papa was somewhat unconventional too. Anyway, he took me back to my friend's house, and we talked for hours. His name is Bill, by the way. Bill Cooper. He is twenty-nine years old, and although it's still early days, let's just say that we are very fond of each other."

It seemed no time at all before Mary Ann gave up her fervent campaigning to spend most of her time with Bill. He became a frequent visitor to the Lee household. The four of them would often spend the evening playing cribbage, chess, or mahjong. Bill lived with his parents and three siblings in a small village a few miles away on the outskirts of the New Forest. His sisters, Margaret and Dorothy, were about the same age as Mary Ann, and the three of them swiftly became great friends. Ben, his brother, was only twelve years old and much too occupied with playing football with his friends or riding out on his bicycle to pay much attention to this new visitor.

Both families owned crystal radio sets and would frequently listen, through the crackling static, to the news of the day. When the miners went on strike in May 1926, Fred pessimistically predicted, "Mark my words, there's trouble on the way." He was a prudent businessman, however, and had taken steps some years before to ensure that his not inconsiderable wealth was protected. He could foresee that many people would find themselves in dire straits and prayed that his own family would weather the storm, promising that he would always help out financially if they needed it.

Fred's gloomy introspection disappeared when Mary Ann announced that Bill had asked her to marry him. "I accepted without a second thought," she said happily. "I've been hoping and planning for weeks and weeks now, and I just can't wait."

Fred and Lizzie were delighted with the news. "So, tell us your plans. When and where?"

"In September," she replied, "at our local church. We're planning to invite all our families, and I should like Susan, Margaret, and

Dorothy to be my bridesmaids. Bill's best friend, Geoff, will act as best man, and Ben will be an usher if he can drag himself away from his football for one day. After the wedding, we thought we could hold a reception at the Thatched Cottage in Brockenhurst."

"Well!" Lizzie laughed. "As you said, you've certainly planned it all in detail."

Once again, Fred and Lizzie found themselves being swept along on a tide of excited planning. When the day finally arrived, they were relieved that everything went well. To her parents' surprise, Mary Ann had decided to be a traditional bride. She wore a long lacy dress with a veil to match, whilst her bridesmaids' gowns were in pale purple. All the women and girls carried bouquets of purple and white flowers interwoven with tiny green leaves. Because many of Mary Ann's friends from the suffragette movement had been invited to the wedding, they appreciated this subtle nod to their cause.

Thirty-nine

Back home after the wedding, Fred relaxed in his favourite armchair and remarked, "That's three down and one to go!"

"Oh, I'd be surprised if Susan marries," Lizzie replied. "She is wedded to her job, and because of the long hours, she really doesn't have much of a social life." Susan, indeed, had fulfilled her dream of becoming a doctor, and her dedication to her work was becoming legendary in the hospital. Whatever the time of day or night, Susan seemed to be there, dispensing wisdom and kindness in equal measure. Having qualified in general medicine, she had now set her sights on specialising in paediatrics.

"After all," Susan quipped, "I am Auntie to so many children that it has surely given me a head start in the subject!" Fred and Lizzie were concerned that their daughter had perhaps taken on too much, but on the rare occasions when she was able to visit, they were relieved to see that she was thriving and happy. By her fortieth birthday, she had become a well-known authority in her chosen profession.

It was with great astonishment and some concern, therefore, that Fred and Lizzie learned that she planned to give it all up to marry a fellow doctor and settle in a run-down practice in London. "His name is Alec," Susan told them, "and he is a widower. He has been working at the hospital for the past few months, and we hit it off right from the beginning. The practice he is taking over is in a sorry state in a rather drab area of London, but it has such great potential, and we are very excited about it." Her eyes shining with enthusiasm, she continued, saying, "The people there really need decent medical support. A lot of them don't have enough money to eat properly, so their health suffers. We are hoping to set up some sort of scheme whereby the patients pay us what they can afford. And if they can't afford anything, then treatment will be offered without charge!"

Fred and Lizzie listened with some consternation. "Are you quite sure?" they asked in chorus. "It will be a hard life, you know."

"Yes, we realise that, but it will be very rewarding, and we are totally committed to this. We can't wait!"

"All we want is for you to be happy," said Lizzie. "If you think you will find happiness and fulfilment in the life you are planning, then you have our total backing. Isn't that so, Fred?"

Fred slowly nodded his head in agreement. "We are very proud of you," he said somewhat gruffly, "and we're looking forward to meeting this man who seems to have turned your life upside down."

"I'm sure you will like him; he is the proverbial tall, dark, and handsome chap, and his patients adore him!"

Susan and Alec were duly married with very little pomp, opting for a ceremony in a registry office near to their new lodgings in London. They promised one another that when they had the time, they would go house-hunting, but in the meantime their small flat was convenient enough.

Forty

Two years had passed, in which Fred and Lizzie lived a very contented life. Fred revived his old love for carpentry, and his family kept him occupied with various commissions which he was delighted to fulfil. He built a swing and a seesaw in the back garden for the amusement of the younger grandchildren, whilst Lizzie took up knitting and produced many warm and comfortable garments for the family. She had also become the proud owner of a Singer sewing machine and discovered she had quite a talent for dressmaking and tailoring. From that time, she finally began to wear shorter skirts and relished the freedom of movement which they gave her. She had always been slender, and now she received many compliments on her new look.

The Lees' old crystal set had long been replaced by a smart Bakelite radio, and they had the *Radio Times* delivered to them weekly so that they could keep in touch with all the entertainment available. Listening to *Henry Hall's Guest Music Night* was a favourite. Fred would often take Lizzie in his arms and whirl her around the living room until they were breathless from both exertion and laughter.

Fred's eightieth birthday loomed ahead of them, and despite protestations that he didn't want a fuss, Lizzie determined to hold a big celebration to honour the occasion. She started planning some weeks before and was delighted when every invitation she sent out was accepted. "Let's see," she had cogitated, "there's our good friends the Leighs and the Evanses, and we mustn't forget the Wrights, although they might not be able to cope with the journey. And the

Harpers. Then, of course, there's the family: Josh, Anique, and their three; Martha, Frank, and all four of their children; Ada, Alfred, and their little one; and last but not least, Mary Ann and Bill plus their family." She had also contacted Sarah and was happy to learn that she and her husband would be honoured to be included. Richard, Fred's business partner and longtime friend, also accepted, despite having himself reached the even greater age of ninety. Sadly, his wife had died some years before, but Richard was still active, visiting his family whenever the opportunity arose and spending a great deal of his time pottering around the garden or hanging around down at the Carpenters Arms, where he still enjoyed a pint with a large circle of friends, young and old.

"You've taken on an awful lot of work there," commented Fred. "Are you sure you can manage?"

"Oh yes," came the confident reply. "Thank goodness we have that great big refrigerator, so I can start preparing some of the food two or three days beforehand. Don't forget, too, that the days will be getting chilly in October, so some of the items can go in the mesh box outside. They will keep fresh there. The secret is to make lists then more lists."

"So, you won't need my help then?" Fred asked, half-joking.

"Goodness, no! You just keep out of my way and let me get on with all the preparations."

"Then I will amuse myself planning a few games for us to play. We can't just sit around and talk all the time or the youngsters will get bored."

Fred happily took himself off to a quiet corner to plan a quiz, and then, having spent a couple of hours devising one that was suitable for both young and old, he went upstairs to delve into one of the cupboards where their old board games were kept. Gleefully, he pulled out packs of cards to play—"Happy Families", "Oh Hell", and canasta—but discarded Monopoly as the game would probably take too long to play. Chess was added to the "maybe" pile, although this could sometimes take up too much time, but Scrabble met with approval. Right at the back of the cupboard, Fred discovered an old box of magic tricks which he had tried to master many years ago to amuse his children. He smiled to himself, remembering that up to the age of five they were suitably mystified, but beyond that age they would shout out, "It's up your sleeve!" or "It's in your pocket!" and were not fooled in the slightest. He made a mental note to buy some prizes—nothing too elaborate, perhaps a few packets of chocolates like Smarties, Rolo, and Maltesers. There would be a few frowns and remarks about "bad for the teeth", but it was only this once.

The family had held secret discussions as to the present they would give their father for this milestone birthday. Despite many ideas, nothing seemed to fit the bill, until Lizzie suggested, "I know he rather fancies a Rolex watch. How about if you all club together to buy one?"

This met with instant approval, and Josh was commissioned to explore all the different possibilities, finally coming up with one which had just come on the market. "It's rather expensive," warned Josh, "but it looks just right. It has a strong leather strap and it's waterproof, which I think will appeal to him."

Indeed, it did appeal to Fred, who appeared overwhelmed to have received such a generous present from his family. He immediately fastened it to his wrist with pride, and it seemed that every two minutes or so he would consult it to ascertain the time. In the end, the grandchildren began to tease him: "What's the time, Grandpa?" or "Is it time for another game, Grandpa?" or "Is it time for tea, Grandpa?" Fred took it all in good heart, being so very happy that he was surrounded by such warmth and love.

Lizzie had performed a near-miracle in providing food for more than thirty people. They couldn't all be seated at the table, but the younger ones were happy to sit on the well-carpeted floor, whilst everybody else settled on a chair with carefully balanced plates on their laps and glasses in their hands. Small pies, sandwiches, and sausage rolls disappeared quickly, to be followed by cakes, biscuits, and cream-filled scones. Everybody declared they had eaten to their fill until the birthday cake arrived, a stupendous three-tiered fruit cake covered with marzipan and icing sugar with the message "Happy

80th Birthday" scrawled across the top in bright red. Representing the eighty years of Fred's life were eight candles because, as Lizzie laughingly explained, "The cake would have had to be a yard across to accommodate eighty candles."

"Blow them all out, Grandpa, and don't forget to make a wish." Fred smilingly complied, but he kept his wish a secret.

Forty-one

One night in November of that same year, the Lees heard the upsetting news that the Crystal Palace had burned down, with a graphic description of the organ groaning as it collapsed into the flames. They had never visited this amazing building but had read a great deal about it over the years and were sad to know that it would no longer either grace the landscape or receive visitors to marvel at its construction or enjoy the exhibitions held there.

Less than two months later, on 11 December, Fred was relaxing in his armchair whilst Lizzie was in the kitchen preparing their lunch when a sudden radio announcement made him sit up straight and call to his wife: "Come in here quickly!" They listened in silence as King Edward VIII made his solemn abdication speech announcing that he was giving up the throne in order to marry Wallis Simpson.

"Well, well!" was Lizzie's reaction. "That was the only reasonable outcome, wasn't it? Who does she think she is? Expecting to marry the King of England and no doubt become his queen! What a nerve!"

"I agree," Fred replied. "The British public would never have accepted her. I feel sorry for the new king, though. Being thrust into the public eye so suddenly must be a real ordeal, and I believe he suffers from a stammer, which will make it very difficult for him. Poor man!"

"He has a very supportive wife," replied Lizzie, "and two gorgeous daughters, so I'm sure he will be a popular and dutiful king. I wonder what will become of Edward and Wallis. Surely they won't be allowed to stay in England now."

"Not our problem," Fred responded cheerfully. "I'm so glad I'm not royal!"

With the approach of Christmas, Fred and Lizzie agreed they would really prefer not to have a big family gathering again quite so soon. Although they had enjoyed his eightieth birthday party enormously, it had taken a lot of their energy. As Lizzie succinctly remarked, "We must remember that we're getting on a bit now, and we can't rush around like we used to do."

"You're quite right," Fred agreed. "I'll be more than happy to spend the day alone with you. We'll let the family know and leave them to make their own arrangements."

"You don't think they will feel hurt by our decision?" Lizzie asked anxiously, only to be reassured.

"Of course not," Fred said definitely. "They will understand."

On Christmas morning, Lizzie walked into her kitchen and momentarily felt a little sad that she wouldn't be bustling around and preparing all the food for her large family. Then she smiled, sat down, and made herself a leisurely cup of tea. Fred soon joined her, and together they sat in companionable silence, looking forward to the day ahead.

"We mustn't forget to listen to the King's speech," said Lizzie.

"There isn't going to be one this year," Fred replied, "because of the abdication. That was only two weeks ago, and I'm sure King George VI has more than enough to contend with at the moment."

"Would you like some breakfast?" enquired Lizzie.

"Just a piece of toast will do. I'm looking forward to my turkey dinner."

"Well, you'll have a long wait, my dear, because I've made a change this year. We're having rolled lamb shoulder stuffed with apples and pine nuts with lots of roast potatoes and vegetables, followed by a clementine and gingerbread trifle."

"Sounds absolutely delicious! You are a wonderful cook, you know, and I'm a very lucky man."

The hours passed peacefully by. Fred and Lizzie enjoyed eating their alternative Christmas dinner, and afterwards they dozed in front of the blazing fire, which Fred had lit earlier. They listened to the radio and laughed out loud at some of the comedy featured, especially Elsie and Doris Waters in their roles as cockney characters Gert and Daisy. "I'd love to meet them," said Lizzie. "I'm sure they would be the most interesting people to talk to."

"I've read that the scientists are experimenting with the idea of bringing pictures to a screen in everyone's living room. It seems quite bizarre, but who knows what the future holds. After all, in our lifetime we have seen some incredible changes, haven't we?" Fred stared into the fire and began to reminisce over his eighty years of life. How lucky he had been! Apart from the *Avalanche* tragedy, he had been so very fortunate in all aspects of his life. He enjoyed a very happy marriage with a wife whom he adored, and he had great pride in his children and grandchildren, whom he loved unconditionally. His business had been very successful, so consequently he had no money worries. Then there was Joshua's miraculous return from the war and Lizzie's recovery from the Spanish flu. So many things to be deeply grateful for.

If he had decided all those years ago to emigrate to New Zealand with his family, Fred thought, then his life would have ended and there would have been nothing.

He gave a great sigh of contentment, and Lizzie gazed enquiringly at him. "Penny for them," she said.

"I was just thinking how very lucky I have been all my life," he replied. "If my dear old dog had not adopted me that day sixty years ago, then none of this would have happened. I almost certainly would have been persuaded to join my ma and pa in their doomed quest for a better life. The fact that I did not go with them on the *Avalanche* was all because of a dog called Lucky."[1]

The End

---

[1] Frederick Lee Senior was my great grandmother's brother. He, his wife Matilda, and his four daughters did indeed drown in the *Avalanche* disaster in 1877. However, Frederick and Matilda did not have a son, so the rest of my story is fiction.

Milton Keynes UK
Ingram Content Group UK Ltd.
UKHW021055150524
442707UK00014B/322

9 781982 288433